The machine gun opened up

Quinn raced across the street and grabbed Ramsey just as a line of automatic fire from the assault drone's .50 caliber gun walked its way across the cobblestones of the street behind her, throwing up a line of yellow sparks. He shoved her forward into the shadows of an alley mouth as another salvo cut him off from the passage.

Flipping sideways, Quinn flattened against the side of a building, gripped the Uzi machine pistol in both hands and aimed at the dark shape circling overhead. Sighting the attack drone and tracking just ahead of its flight trajectory, he squeezed off a burst of 9 mm parabellums.

The fire was accurate.

The steeljackets stitched the drone aircraft across the sensitive visionic pod situated in its nose assembly. Now operating without any guidance system to stabilize its flight, the aircraft began to weave crazily in the night sky.

NOMAD

DAVID ALEXANDER

A GOLD EAGLE BOOK FROM

WORLDWIDE.

TORONTO • NEW YORK • LONDON
AMSTERDAM • PARIS • SYDNEY • HAMBURG
STOCKHOLM • ATHENS • TOKYO • MILAN
MADRID • WARSAW • BUDAPEST • AUCKLAND

If you purchased this book without a cover you should be aware
that this book is stolen property. It was reported as "unsold and
destroyed" to the publisher, and neither the author nor the
publisher has received any payment for this "stripped book."

*Except where specifically noted or contextually
apparent, all references to weapons and/or
combat systems and technologies now in use refer
to next-generation versions thereof.*

First edition April 1992

ISBN 0-373-62115-9

NOMAD

Copyright © 1992 by David Alexander.
Philippine copyright 1992. Australian copyright 1992.

All rights reserved. Except for use in any review, the
reproduction or utilization of this work in whole or in part
in any form by any electronic, mechanical or other means,
now known or hereafter invented, including xerography,
photocopying and recording, or in any information storage
or retrieval system, is forbidden without the permission
of the publisher, Worldwide Library, 225 Duncan Mill Road,
Don Mills, Ontario, Canada M3B 3K9.

All the characters in this book have no existence outside the
imagination of the author and have no relation whatsoever to
anyone bearing the same name or names. They are not even
distantly inspired by any individual known or unknown to the
author, and all the incidents are pure invention.

® are Trademarks registered in the United States Patent and
Trademark Office and in other countries.

Printed in U.S.A.

The mass and majesty of this world, all
   That carries weight and always weighs the same
Lay in the hands of others; they were small
   And could not hope for help and no help came:
   What their foes liked to do was done, their
      shame
Was all the worst could wish; they lost their pride
And died as men before their bodies died.

      —W. H. Auden
      "The Shield of Achilles"

PROLOGUE

Singapore, A.D. 2030

Kim Sung set down his drink at the bar and idly glanced at the lounge singer in the slinky dress who was belting out the usual tasteless rendition of an American pop tune. His own people, Kim had realized after many years spent in the United States, knew nothing about American popular culture. Nevertheless they insisted on doing their best to imitate it every chance they got.

The drink was the raunchy American sour mash whiskey that Kim had acquired a taste for during his student days at Cal Tech, but right now the bourbon wasn't doing much for the nuclear physicist's state of mind. The depression he felt had been sudden and uncharacteristic. Kim had at first attributed its onset to a kind of postpartum emotional syndrome.

His involvement with the Prometheus Project had consumed his mental and physical energies for the past five years. Small wonder, Kim had acknowledged, that he would feel the shock of let-down now that his role in the project was complete. Kim had decided to take a vacation. However, even after several weeks enjoying the gaming tables and energetic prostitutes of Monte Carlo, his depression had continued to mount.

Now, on his return to Singapore, Kim plunged himself into a new project, hoping that in time his spirits would lift. So far, though, this hadn't happened.

Kim left the bar and found his car, a brand-new Mercedes Tiger, in the lot out front. He gunned the ignition and felt the high-performance engine come to life with a roar as fearsome as that of the automobile's animal namesake. Kim tooled out onto the road that switchbacked above the South China Sea toward his mountaintop villa on the rocky heights that overlooked the ocean.

When he reached the highest point of the steeply winding road, Kim pulled the car over to the shoulder and sat there staring blankly at the sea glittering in the sunlight at the foot of the cliff. Moments later Kim was rolling forward again. He had stopped the car at the last few hundred feet of a straightaway before it became a deadman's curve over a seventy-foot plunge.

Kim's foot smashed down on the gas pedal while his hands gripped the wheel with knuckle-whitening tension. The Mercedes crashed through the metal barrier strip and sailed straight off into empty space.

Moments later it slammed head-on into a rock ledge projecting from the escarpment below. It did a complete flip, coasted in free-fall, then plowed upside down into the boulders on the beach.

Acid from the ruptured fuel cell splashed across bare wire leads. A spark caught the fumes of partially combusted gas rising from the choke. In a pulse beat, the Mercedes and its driver were both consumed in a towering fireball of incinerating flame.

UNTER DEN LINDEN was thronged with its usual assortment of tourists, hustlers, pimps and pickpockets. Since its unification at the beginning of the 1990s, Berlin, the once-proud capital of Germany, had regained most of its former splendor.

While in the cold-war years architecture in the German Democratic Republic had taken on the facelessness typical of postwar Soviet Bloc buildings, much of the structures of old Berlin had been saved in the East and had never been torn down due to the bankrupt Communist government. Now they had been restored.

Fritz Geistmann was emerging from a conference at a chemical firm that had just contracted him to do consulting work. Although he didn't need the money, the compulsion to work was in his blood. After his involvement with Prometheus, nothing else would ever seem as important, but Geistmann's restless mind required constant stimulation. He had taken the assignment more for its therapeutic value than anything else.

It was a beautiful morning. The chemical engineer decided to walk down the Unter den Linden at least part of the distance toward his flat on the Rosa Luxemburg Platz.

As he proceeded on his way, Geistmann reflected on the Nazi Reich that had come of age in this quarter of the ancient capital. Its Prussian architecture still chilled him to the bone. The place hadn't lost the power to conjure up ghosts of a bygone era. Geistmann was a Jew, and the crimes of Nazi Germany against his people had left indelible marks on their collective psyches. But at last the country's instrumental role in the Prometheus Project would free it from its dark shadow and make it resemble its mythological namesake, Prometheus, who stole the gift of fire from the gods and brought it down to humanity.

On a whim Geistmann decided to ride the U-Bahn the rest of the way to his apartment. The electric trains were clean and free of the graffiti that had plagued them before unification. Geistmann stood on the platform and opened the newspaper he had purchased at the kiosk on the mezzanine level of the subway.

Minutes later the pretty young schoolteacher standing beside him let out a bloodcurdling scream as she was splattered with Geistmann's blood.

Geistmann had thrown the paper to the floor just as the U-Bahn train roared into the station. Eyewitnesses all agreed that the man in the gray tweed overcoat had casually stepped into the path of the oncoming express at the last second before it would have streaked past.

A passenger pulled the emergency cord that stopped the U-Bahn train, and the row of cars came screeching to a halt. Commuter traffic was held up for several hours as police and emergency service units labored to retrieve the mangled body parts that had been strewn across the tracks.

All accounts of the incident agreed that the dead man hadn't fallen or been pushed, nor had Geistmann uttered a word that might have explained his actions before he committed suicide. He had simply stepped in front of the oncoming train as naturally as if he were boarding an escalator and been instantly killed.

THE TIME-STAINED BUILDING overlooked the Charles Bridge. It had been built long before the beginning of World War II, in a time when Prague was still known as the armory of Eastern Europe and one of its principal cultural centers. Now, decades after the Czechs had freed themselves from the twin evils of Nazi and then Soviet domination, Prague was again something like the city she had once been.

Inside the spacious drawing room Vlados Havlecek entertained his many guests. The expert on laser-based guidance systems was celebrating his forty-sixth birthday with a gala party. This occasion was doubly auspicious because it also marked the conclusion of many years of work on the Prometheus Project's guidance components, critical to the performance of the sophisticated hardware.

Havlecek looked a bit drawn, but his guests attributed the signs of stress to the scientist's dedication to making Prometheus a reality, efforts that the world media had brought to every Czech's attention during the many phases of the ambitious project.

The salon of the scientist's villa became hushed as servants wheeled in a magnificent birthday cake, its frosted top bedecked with an array of burning candles.

As they stared at the cake, few noticed Havlecek calmly walk toward one of the high windows and quickly cross to the edge of the balcony that fronted the villa. Those guests who saw his face just before he leaped to his death on the ancient cobbles of the Charles Bridge below related that the scientist's expression was completely blank, bearing no trace of emotion whatsoever.

THE ANCIENT LITANY droned in the killer's ears. Genesis had paid twenty thousand U.S. dollars to participate in the age-old ceremony among the Perdoni of Taranto's Easter Pageant.

Their faces hooded, huge crosses of heavy wood cradled in their arms, the Perdoni walked less than two miles across Taranto from dusk of Good Friday until dawn of Easter Sunday, advancing by tiny steps in emulation of Christ's last trek toward Golgotha.

The pain was excruciating. It was said that only the chosen few granted special grace could bear it.

Genesis hadn't been born into the faith. The killer had discovered the strange ritual completely by accident after terminating an arms dealer in Cairo.

The hit had been carried out perfectly. The arms dealer's death had involved mutilations characteristic of the Muslim Brotherhood. The shipment of small arms that he had been brokering in a complex scam involving the covert intelligence networks of three nations had been thrown into complete disarray.

The arms shipment had been successfully diverted to Alpha's ground assets in preparation for the coming operation. However, with each of the three nations busy pointing fingers at one another, Alpha would never be suspected as the principal behind the murder or the theft.

But for Genesis something had changed after the Cairo strike. For the first time Genesis hadn't felt the exhilaration that had always come with the large payment to a numbered Swiss account and the knowledge of a flawlessly executed assignment. For the first time Genesis had felt the gnawing of a strange new emotion. *Conscience.*

Conscience was a dangerous thing to carry around in the business Genesis was in. For Genesis conscience was a slowly ticking bomb.

In Paris there were houses of bondage where surgically altered women could bring sublime forgetfulness through the precise infliction of pleasure and pain. Genesis had drunk of the dark pleasures they offered to the full, had drifted perilously close to the ragged edge of insanity. But not even there could he find tranquillity.

In the Taranto Easter Pageant the assassin had immediately sensed the promise of redemption. Money had been no object. For twice the asking price Genesis had purchased a position among the Perdoni and, through the excruciating ordeal of walking the Stations of the Cross, been purged of the madness that had been lurking nearby.

Afterward, Genesis could kill again. Precisely, efficiently. With the ticking bomb of conscience finally defused.

Taranto had then become a regular ritual. A yearly atonement. A cleansing of the killer's soul.

Genesis had been slowly crossing the town's cobblestone streets in bare feet since sunset of the night before. Almost immediately Genesis had lapsed into a trancelike state in which time stood still and became an eternity washed by a warm sea of milky white light.

Suddenly there came the sound of chanting. The procession halted. The leader of the procession knocked three times on the bolted portals of the town cathedral. The huge oaken doors swung ponderously open.

Genesis followed the Perdoni inside the cathedral. Washed in the blood of the Lamb, Genesis was redeemed.

Now Genesis could kill again.

MISSION LOG ONE:

Probe

1

Darkness shrouded the desert launch facility of Orbital Systems Technologies. The night was moonless, and starlight was the only source of illumination. Elapsed mission time: 002 minutes.

Shadows cloaked the striker as he advanced on the target. His mission: hard penetration, ultimate destruction.

The night-black stealthsuit worn by the striker fitted snugly over his muscular body, elasticized to give as he moved, with no tags or buckles to snag at a dangerous moment. Gloves of a thin polymerized material encased his hands, the head was cowled, and high-topped, ripple-soled boots protected his feet.

The thin profile of a virtual-reality goggles—VRG—device resembling a diver's mask projected from his face, which was cammied in heat-dissipating stripes of nonreflective black combat paint.

A network of microthin plastic tubes sandwiched between the fabric of the stealthsuit crisscrossed every inch of the shadow warrior's body.

Temperature-diffusing gases constantly circulated through the artificial capillaries of the dark-hued action togs to create a mixed pattern of hot and cold as thermal camouflage.

Even the most sensitive TI—thermal-imaging—sensors used by conventional night vision equipment would have extreme difficulty in detecting the heat signature of the operative in the suit. Personal stealth technology had finally given the techno-commando a power that had always been the stuff of myth: invisibility.

Quinn was the striker's name. Quinn and nothing else. He had stopped using his first name years before, rejecting it as irrelevant. He had also dropped the code name he had used during his hitch with Scepter. Nomad was a handle out of another life as far as Quinn was concerned.

The VRG device worn by Quinn was a revolutionary piece of precision combat gear in its own right. Its multiple sensor array incorporated TI, IR—infrared—and II—image-intensification—visionics and sensorics.

Invisible, Q-switched, neodymium-doped YAG laser beams selectively painted the op zone, illuminating details invisible to both the unaided eye and conventional night-observation devices.

All input was filtered through ultra high-speed microprocessors hard-wired into the VRGs' 686-based CPU. The result was a multimode eyes-up display of sharp resolution.

Tiger duty was the subject of tonight's mission profile. Covert penetration of the hard perimeter and implantation of a compact SADM, a Special Atomic Demolition Munition, that was, in effect, a very small but very deadly nuclear bomb. Base personnel were to be taken down in the process.

Quick in, quick out.

No prisoners.

No excuses.

Quinn reached the fifteen-foot-high perimeter fence that surrounded the base. There he froze, probing passively, for the present letting the hardware do the grunt work. In zoom mode the VRG raster's graphical user interface displayed the entire expanse of the installation, showing him the concrete blockhouses, Quonset huts and launch gantries that sprawled across the quarter mile of open desert.

Quinn's passive scan continued. He shifted to schematic overlay, and another sweep flashed him a glowing three-dimensional wire grid map pinpointing the array of TI and LLTV—low-light television—perimeter sensors linked to the base command center. These passive sensors would issue a silent intruder alarm when triggered by the appropriate threat configuration.

Quinn wasn't overly concerned about the perimeter sensors. The stealthsuit and VRG combo could defeat these. But buried in the sand there were probably motion sensors, too—perhaps linked to area denial submunitions—which his equipment couldn't so easily detect, and these needed bypassing.

Quinn moved quickly between the blind spots of the swiveling LLTV cameras. Using shears of an ultrahard nonmetallic polymer, he snipped out a section of the perimeter fence.

Replacing the cutout section with plastic ties to minimize the risk of detection once he was inside the fence, Quinn scanned the terrain ahead through his VRGs. Invisible lasers picked up the faint traces of buried motion sensor pods that unaided human eyes couldn't distinguish.

The cordon of hidden motion sensors was arrayed just within the fence, attuned to the body mass of anything larger and heavier than a coyote. Stepping carefully, Quinn avoided these.

Six minutes into the mission, Quinn encountered the first Orbital Systems security guard walking his perimeter. The uniformed guard passed by without taking notice of him as Quinn crouched in the darkness.

Although the guard, too, was equipped with night vision goggles, the binocular lenses of the sentry's passive infrared NVGs were blind to Quinn's presence. Well diffused by the stealth-suit, Quinn's heat signature couldn't be detected by the NVGs worn by the guard.

Invisible in the shadows, Quinn remained perfectly motionless until the guard continued past his position. Then, breaking from cover, Quinn crouch-walked toward the site of the base's radar-tracking module.

The schematic map display showing the module's location was already preprogrammed into the VRG's random access memory and his eyes-up display depicted another three-dimensional wire diagram that led him directly toward it. All Quinn had to do was follow the flashing yellow line of dashes on the eyes-up display and he was home free.

Quinn was almost at his designated target site when another guard suddenly rounded the corner of a large fuel storage tank and popped up directly in front of him. The uniformed security man was startled by the dark, looming mass but moved fast, raising the black bullpup serial flechette rifle he ported as his night vision goggles gained focus on the intruder, now close enough to be visible as a faint, glimmering man shape in his glowing electronic view field.

Quinn was moving, too, reacting much faster than the surprised guard, pulling the advanced-design weapon from his breakaway chest rig with the faint rasp of Velcro fastenings disengaging.

The doughnut-shaped close-assault weapon clutched in his fists was comprised of durable high-impact plastic. The FN P90 close-assault weapon might resemble an oversize doughnut equipped with a plastic stock, but it was a lethal firearm that delivered more than three times the terminal ballistics of a conventional SMG. Silencer-equipped, the P90 made hardly any sound as it discharged a three-round autoburst of needle-nosed 5.70x28 mm rounds and softly ejected the spent casings through a port situated at the bottom of the ambidextrous weapon's frame.

The high-velocity rounds scored a tight pattern in the center of the target's chest. The sentry went down with a grunt and lay motionless on the ground.

Reholstering the P90, the covert penetrator moved on, following the broken line on his strike management raster interface.

Nine minutes into the mission Quinn reached the nerve center of the launch facility. The flashing broken lines on his goggles' display now resolved into a glowing three-dimensional cube superimposed over an icon representing the phased-array radar installation that was essential to tracking and controlling the various pieces of orbital hardware the company launched into space for its international clients.

With a short beep tone in his ear, the VRGs indicated that Quinn had reached the mission's target site programmed into its volatile memory. Again there was the rasp of Velcro surfaces disengaging as Quinn unshipped the special ordnance he'd brought with him from a pouch riding ALICE webbing on his back.

The special atomic demolition munition or SADM had been engineered down to the dimensions of an oversize thermos jug, which it resembled more closely than anything else except for its mat-black finish, the recessed carrying handle on its side and the words M/2A Subkiloton Thermonuclear Explosive Device stenciled in white across its middle.

A metal stirrup or "church key" was inserted into a locking mechanism in its top and turned counterclockwise, activating a microprocessor chip that placed the SADM in standby mode.

A keypad just below the carrying handle was used to program precise settings into the nuke's computer CMOS ROM chip, alphanumerics that were flashed on a backlit LCD display above the keypad. A final twist of the church key armed the micronuke.

Once armed, its automatic fail-safe program would defeat any attempts to neutralize the SADM. Thanks to its sophisticated detection circuitry, tampering with the nuke beyond this point would trigger it into going critical. The nuke would detonate, one way or the other, and nothing this side of hell could prevent it.

Quinn set the SADM's timer and quickly withdrew from ground zero. He was soon back where he'd started, outside the snipped-out section of security fence soon thereafter, with an elapsed mission time of just under fourteen minutes.

As Quinn pulled the VRGs from his head, a powerful helium-arc spotlight flashed suddenly to life, pinning Quinn in its cyclopean glare.

Quinn shaded his eyes as he squinted into the blinding light source. Centered in the glare, a dark man shape was approaching him at a slow amble.

A smile crossed Quinn's lean, hard features. He continued to stare into the light as the figure approached him.

"Damn fine job," the gruff voice of Orbital Systems' security chief said as he stuck out his hand. Quinn grasped the callused hand and shook hard. "There's a bottle of not half-bad whiskey in my office," the security chief went on. "Let's you and me have a belt while we review the mission specs."

Quinn and the security chief turned and walked out of the light.

2

Art Raxwell, chief of base security of Colorado's Orbital Systems Technologies, sat in the truck loaded with high-tech equipment. Quinn was already programming the data for postmission analysis into his palmtop computer.

"You sure punched a hole in our security cordon," Raxwell told him, shaking his head. "I wouldn't have believed anybody could do it."

"Don't sweat it, Raxwell," Quinn returned, swiveling in his chair to face the graying ex-cop. "Your system wasn't bad. It just wasn't geared to take on the latest technology. Better for me to find and plug the holes than for some terrorist head cases to do it for you."

Raxwell nodded, glad that he had opted for Quinn to test the base defenses despite the company bigwigs' reservations. Had a genuine terrorist unit penetrated the base and planted an operational SADM instead of the dummy Quinn had used, the consequences would have been more than just disastrous for Orbital. If a nuclear disaster had occurred, then the whole tristate area could have been hit.

Terrorist International was no longer unsophisticated. Its members were now dedicated, well trained and well equipped. Small, cheap, accurate and readily available weapons systems made a single man as deadly as an entire strike force from a previous era.

The high-visibility ops that had been characteristic of the late twentieth century had long since been dropped in favor of well-planned, precision-executed surgical strikes in pursuit of often complex political objectives.

Terror had come of age.

"How long before you can give me the specs on the new plan?" Raxwell asked Quinn. "My chief of operations will be ready to take a rusty razor to my balls when he finds out how quick you got in and planted the nuke."

"Fax you the full data and recommendations by tomorrow afternoon," Quinn told Raxwell as he snapped his palmtop shut and packed up his gear. Now, dressed in street clothes, a black leather jacket, six-pocket pants and high-topped sneakers, Quinn walked with the security chief toward the asphalt parking lot.

On the way to his high-performance Sunhawk, Quinn passed the security guard he had "taken out" on his penetration run, recognizing the effects of high-energy ammo on the shredded flak vest the man was now inspecting. The lightweight flak vest worn under his uniform had stopped the P90 rounds cold. Quinn flashed the guy a thumbs-up, and the guard waved back fast before turning away.

Quinn couldn't blame the guy for feeling sullen. He'd be black and blue for a week after being hit by the deflected 5.70s. Quinn would make certain his report would contain a recommendation that no disciplinary action be taken against the security operative. The Orbital employee had been doing his job well and had been surprised due to a system that required upgrading, not because of any dereliction in the performance of his assigned duties.

Raxwell turned to head back, and Quinn slid behind the wheel of the sleek, gull-winged vehicle, punching in his security code on the dashboard. If he didn't, then the car was programmed to lock its doors automatically, and subject whatever unauthorized party had gotten in to a series of nasty surprises, including knockout gas that would paralyze a car booster for several hours.

Sometime later Quinn pulled into the underground parking garage of the high-rise hotel in Denver where Orbital had booked him a room. A figure emerged from behind a concrete support beam and walked toward him across the deserted car park.

"How's it going, kemo sabe?"

The voice had a rasp like sandpaper on broken glass.

The figure extended his hand and waited.

Quinn swung the carryall containing his gear out of the Sunhawk and walked toward the figure, not saying a word. The guy was almost as tall as he, standing a full six feet. He had a barrel chest and massive arms, but his midsection had long ago run to suet. His face had a red, permanently flushed look to it and his long jaw was marred by a pale pink scar that ran down his throat and disappeared beneath the turtleneck collar of his shirt.

Quinn remembered the night mission during which he had received that scar. He and the stranger went back a long way. He also remembered that he hated the guy's guts. Quinn ignored the offered handshake and walked past the figure.

"This is important, kemo sabe," the stranger said, falling into step beside Quinn, who headed for the elevator bank straight ahead of them. "Listen to me, damn it!" The big man placed his hand on Quinn's shoulder, meaning to spin him around.

It was a mistake.

With astonishing speed Quinn pivoted on his left foot and jacked his balled right fist into the big man's solar plexus. There was plenty of steam behind the punch, and the big man wheezed and staggered backward. His face drained of blood as he gasped for air. His attaché case thudded to the concrete.

Quinn turned and watched the big man flop around on the floor like a beached whale. His eyes teared with pain and his face went livid. He held his stomach and tried to regain his balance.

Quinn smiled mirthlessly.

Some of the tension that had been building in his body at the sight of the man drained from him now. He didn't offer to help the guy he'd just decked get to his feet. He just stood over the struggling man and watched impassively.

"Son of a bitch," the big guy spluttered, propping himself against the side of a car. "You miserable bastard. You didn't have to do that."

"I felt like doing it," Quinn said softly, a steel edge in his voice.

He felt like doing it again, in fact. He took a step forward and raised his right leg as if to deliver a kick to the downed man's face.

The stranger sensed what was coming, sensed the depth of the hatred Quinn felt for him. He put up his hands in a defensive gesture as he rose to his feet, then dropped them to his aching belly again.

"You won't get rid of me," he told Quinn, clutching his hurt midsection. "This is serious business. I know you hate my guts, and I don't blame you, bucko, but I've got authorization from the highest levels."

Quinn looked the fat man over for a long time. "Who exactly do you mean?"

"The President of the United States," the newcomer responded with a wheeze.

"Tomorrow morning, Bruckner. Nine sharp. My office," Quinn said after a moment's pause. Then he turned and punched the elevator button.

The elevator doors closed behind him. The big man shook his head, picked up his dropped attaché case and walked back to a car parked at the other end of the lot.

Inside the car somebody else waited, face hidden in the shadows, having witnessed the entire incident.

"You get a good look?" Bruckner asked, still wheezing from the fiery pain in his stomach.

"Yes," replied the one in the passenger seat. "Yes, he is most impressive."

"Better believe it, kemo sabe," Bruckner said as he gunned the ignition and screamed the car up one of the sloping ramps of the concrete mausoleum. "Just don't fuck up, or he'll waste us both."

"You needn't worry," Genesis said flatly. "I won't."

QUINN SAT ACROSS the desk from Wild Bill Bruckner in his office at Intervention Systems, the one-man security firm he ran. The man from Quinn's past had arrived promptly at IS. He had brought some audiovisuals with him. The high-definition TV screen on Quinn's office wall sprang to life as the video images flashed across it.

The images were shocking.

"That's Kim," Bruckner explained. "He was the first to get it. His body was burned to charcoal in the wreckage of his car, so there was a limit to what forensics could determine."

Bruckner fast-forwarded to more video cutaway. In rapid succession Quinn watched a grim montage of the aftermath of the violent deaths of men in Prague, Berlin, Rome, Paris, New York and Jerusalem.

"Any pattern to these?" Quinn asked, transfixed by the on-screen visuals.

"None that we can determine. They've been happening over the past couple of months. Needless to say, intelligence and law enforcement have muzzled the media as much as possible."

And done a good job, too, Quinn mentally added. Quinn had seen reports of some of the deaths, and the media accounts had stated that all the scientists associated with the Prometheus Net had committed suicide and experts doubted that there was any connection.

The people who had sent Bruckner had indeed done a good job of keeping a lid on what had been happening. He was now beginning to understand why they had sent Bruckner to find him.

The pattern of homicides meant that Wilhelm Koenig, the director of the Prometheus development group was also marked for death. Koenig was a hero to the world, his presence drawing billions of dollars in grants and donations to the venture. If he died, then the project might die with him.

"Where do I fit into the picture?" Quinn asked Bruckner.

"Nomad was the best," Bruckner told Quinn as the audiovisuals stopped and the screen blanked. "I ought to know. I helped make you."

"I'm not Nomad anymore," Quinn told him, a dangerous edge coming suddenly into his voice. "I'm just Quinn—businessman, security specialist and pillar of society. Scepter doesn't run me. I don't take any orders from you or anybody else, Bruckner."

Quinn's thoughts turned back to his years with the covert agency called Scepter.

Low-intensity conflicts—known to the military as LICs—both overt and covert, major and minor, were fought. Scepter had been signed into being by a covert presidential finding of the late 1990s. Scepter was tasked to deploy every means to deal with terrorism in all its multifarious forms. Its agents were outfitted with the latest high-tech equipment and given a mandate to go out and kick ass.

Then something had gone wrong.

Scepter had become corrupt, a constituent of the selfsame evil it had come into being to combat.

Partly from greed, partly from the corruption that comes with almost limitless power, the men at the top were cooperating in a perpetuation of the bloody status quo ante. Quinn found out about the conspiracy that kept the shadow war alive while ground assets and civilians alike died in pursuit of its twisted aims. Locked into a vicious, perpetual cycle of kill and counterkill, there was no way out.

Quinn himself managed to escape from Scepter. He succeeded in gathering enough intel on the inner circle of dispassionate manipulators who ran the organization to keep himself safe from their retribution.

Bruckner had been one of those unprincipled manipulators, one of the inner circle of the corrupt. Bruckner had been the head of Scepter's elite Directorate One.

His moon face had a permanently florid complexion, which made him appear as though he was always recovering from a hangover or had just stepped out of a sauna. Cold blue eyes looked out of that red moon face. Crazy eyes.

At first glance Bruckner was an unlikely choice to head the Central Intelligence Agency as DCI, and later, the deep-cover counterterror unit called Scepter. But then again, as Quinn knew all to well, picking unlikely candidates for the director's post was almost a tradition at the Agency. Bruckner's two namesakes, "Wild Bills" Donovan and Casey, were two cases in point.

The first was a loose cannon, a guy who, according to Company legend, had once demonstrated a new silenced autopistol just in from the lab by firing it in the Oval Office while the President was speaking on the phone. The second was an absentminded professor type from Queens, who was unconnected with the realities of the world.

But superficial details aside, all three Wild Bills were effective at what they did, adept at navigating through the wilderness of mirrors that was the domain of covert operations. All three had earned their nicknames by daredevil stunts and a cowboy operational philosophy that produced concrete results where cooler heads had failed.

Bruckner's handling of the Snake River Crisis was a case in point. The covert team he'd sent into the nuclear launch facility had used banned nerve agents to kill the terrorists who had taken it over and threatened to launch the aging ICBMs at targets both in the U.S. and Russia.

It was in the aftermath of this successful if controversial strike that the President had signed another covert finding granting Scepter an even broader mandate in the counterterrorist offensive.

Quinn had been a member of Delta when Bruckner chose him to be part of Scepter's elite Directorate One.

Bruckner had taken Quinn and made him into what he became for Scepter—a human killing machine. Bruckner had seen his lethal talent in the sands of the Iraqi desert during the covert action of the 1991 campaign and molded him into a member of an elite strike crew. As the point man of a highly mobile Special Forces unit, Quinn had worked behind the scenes, gathering intelligence and carrying out strategic hits that had helped score a lightning victory for the American-led Coalition.

During his years with Scepter, Quinn was sent into the hardzones of the new counterterrorist combat environment. The emerging world order had need of men such as him. His identity had been submerged in that of his code name.

Nomad.

Quinn became the desert wanderer that his alias suggested, traveling to covert firezones across the globe, doing Scepter's bidding.

"You've got to become Nomad again, kemo sabe," Bruckner told him, abruptly bringing him back to the present. "Just one more time."

3

The hypersonic scramjet's tires screeched onto the runway at Rome's Ciampino International. The pilot applied reverse thrust, and the advanced design turbines screamed in protest as rumble strips further slowed the aircraft's forward momentum. Soon the needle-nosed space plane slowed to a halt and taxied toward the passenger terminal.

The suborbital shuttle run from Washington, D.C., to Rome had taken a little less than an hour with the scramjet's circumpolar flight path skimming the near edge of space.

Quinn's only regret was that there wasn't enough time to watch a full-length in-flight movie, as in the days before space-plane air travel. Quinn himself rarely suffered from jet lag, but the stresses of hypersonic travel made many travelers long for the good old days of supersonic transcontinental flight.

His sole piece of carry-on luggage consisting of the barrel bag that he pulled from beneath his seat, Quinn smiled at the female flight attendant who stood by the forward hatch and was soon walking into the crowded passenger terminal at Ciampino. Continuing past the check-in desks and videophone kiosks, he walked to the gate where he hailed one of the taxis waiting outside.

Some things never changed.

The Italian taxi driver peeled out with a screech of tires and a shouted oath at his fellow hacks. Once on the Rome-Naples highway, he drove with near-suicidal abandon, turning off the highway ten minutes later to career down the narrow Appian Way toward downtown Rome.

In the back seat of the speeding cab Quinn rubbed his tired eyes, beginning to feel the one-two punch of the sudden change in time zones and the lingering effects of hypersonic air travel. He decided to phone the contact, somebody called Ramsey, who Bruckner had said would be waiting to meet him in Rome without further delay.

Reaching into the pocket of his black leather jacket, Quinn took out his phone. He punched the macro key on the keypad of the palmtop wide-area cellular phone that automatically dialed the number he had programmed into the phone's memory. He idly watched the scenery stream past—stubble fields and crumbling stone walls concealing opulent villas from the road with the skyline of Rome in the distance.

"Pronto," a female voice answered on the first ring.

"This is Quinn," he told her. "I'm calling to confirm our meeting."

Switching to English, the female voice on the other end told Quinn to wait a second, and he heard the sounds of computer keys clicking softly in the background.

"How'd your voice analysis check out?" he asked after a moment's pause.

"Perfectly, Mr. Quinn," the female voice countered. "I can meet you any time you wish today. There have been some new developments I'd like to inform you of."

"Fine," Quinn told her, thinking that she sounded about as lively as a computer chip, typical of the kind of individuals he'd worked with while part of Bruckner's crew.

By and large they were emotionless, men and women who could snuff out human lives without feeling the slightest twinge of remorse, messengers of death dressed in the business suits of the new corporate world order and armored with its moral justifications. Quinn had started out as one of Bruckner's zombies, but he had finally found his soul.

"There still a place called Romero's on the Piazza Navona?" Quinn asked, returning to consideration of the business at hand.

"Yes, indeed there is, Mr. Quinn."

"Okay. Meet me there at—" he checked the LCD readout on the phone "—four sharp. I'll tell the maître d' to expect you."

After Bruckner's liaison asset hung up, Quinn dialed the number of the Rafael and made sure his reservations were in order. The deskman told him that they were.

He also informed Quinn that a package was waiting for him. It had arrived via special courier. Quinn slipped the phone back into his pocket and settled into the cushions of the seat as the driver leaned on the horn, narrowly avoiding a head-on collision with a truck in the oncoming lane, and stuck his hand out the window to flash the driver a universal gesture of contempt.

QUINN PEELED OFF a couple of thousand-lira notes and exited the cab. The driver said, *"Grazie, signore,"* and drove away. As he turned toward the hotel entrance, Quinn didn't see him signal to a car parked on the other side of the small square that fronted the hotel.

Inside the car sat two men with hard faces and expressionless eyes. The pair watched Quinn enter the hotel. As he disappeared inside, one of them took a secure phone from his pocket, punched in a priority-coded number and began speaking to a voice thousands of miles away.

AFTER HE SIGNED IN, Quinn was handed the package by the deskman, who first glanced at the faxed color photo of the American beneath the top of the counter and then at the photo on his passport, making sure both matched the face of the guest.

The package turned out to be the special equipment that Quinn had insisted Bruckner provide him with. In his room he checked to make sure the seals that had been applied by CIA handlers were intact. Everything checked out, but Quinn had entertained few doubts of this.

The Rafael had a long history of involvement with Western intelligence agencies and had been used as a CIA safe house on more than one occasion. The hotel staff knew better than to tamper with packages that had been placed in their care.

Quinn showered, then pulled open the wide windows and let in the afternoon air. His room faced west, and Quinn could see the dome of St. Peter's Basilica and the Tiber River glittering in the distance.

Although it was still light, a swarm of incredibly agile chimney swifts darted around the eaves of a time-stained church across the narrow alley that ran beneath the window.

There was a knock at the door.

"Mi scusi, signore," the chambermaid said as Quinn let her in. "I have only to do the bathroom," she added. She was an old woman with a sagging face and she clutched a handful of towels and small packets of soap.

"Prego," Quinn told her and went back to looking out the window as the chambermaid went into the bathroom. He heard her humming a tune as she busied herself with her chores.

Quinn didn't see her slide the long, stubby snout of a sound-suppressed Walther semiautomatic from beneath her apron as she placed the folded towels neatly atop the toilet commode, then pivot toward the room, still humming pleasantly.

Quinn turned just as a subsonic round embedded itself in the woodwork a fraction of an inch from the side of his head. Razor-sharp splinters of spinning wood cut the skin at the corner of his eye.

Quinn reacted instantly, ducking beneath the line of fire even as a second round whizzed past his head. He caught sight of the chambermaid clutching the silenced weapon in the two-handed shooting stance of a professional executioner.

Rolling to one side, Quinn grabbed one of the heavy ashtrays on the dresser and hurled it at the shooter. His aim was accurate. The one-pound lump of glass struck her gun hand, and she let go of the weapon with an anguished cry of pain.

Quinn moved quickly toward the killer in the chambermaid uniform, but the woman was agile and knew how to deal with sudden setbacks. She moved much faster than her aged appearance would indicate, and Quinn suspected her looks were the result of an expert job of disguise.

From a concealed spring-loader in her sleeve, a knife popped into her open hand. She faced him with the naked blade glinting in the light as she waved it back and forth.

She displayed no trace of fear.

Just the opposite.

A mad gleam of almost sexual anticipation lit up her green eyes. Quinn knew there were poisons that could coat the tip of a blade, fast-acting neurotoxins like Tabun or Soman that would be lethal with only a single nick of the blade.

Quinn took the female shiv artist seriously. He gave the woman a wide berth as she advanced, whipping the blade back and forth in deft side-to-side motions.

"You've hurt me," she whispered in a hoarse rasp that betrayed neither youth nor age. "I'll make you pay for that." The woman's voice was no longer accented. It was flat and middle-American.

Thrusting her hand outward from her hip, she lunged suddenly at Quinn with the blade's cutting edge facing away from her, the classic knife fighter's death swipe. Quinn leaped backward as the razor tip of the knife sliced through the fabric of his shirt.

In the confined space of the hotel room Quinn had no illusions about eluding a trained knife fighter. Since speed meant more than power when using a knife, a woman could be as lethal a killer with a blade as any man. Quinn knew that his only chance to survive was to counterattack, move as fast as the woman did.

As she sprang forward with the knife describing a gleaming arc, he ducked low and came up under the silvery line of death. Before she could follow through with another, more accurate strike, Quinn caught hold of her wrist and squeezed with fingers as strong as steel cable.

The woman shrieked with pain, and Quinn felt the delicate wrist bones snap like dry twigs. The knife clattered from her hand, and they collapsed onto the bed in a tangled heap of flailing arms and thrashing legs.

She was incredibly strong, and despite her injured hand there was still plenty of fight left in her. She reached up with her good hand, and Quinn felt her squeeze his windpipe with all her might. His vision dimmed momentarily as he gasped for breath, and he had no choice but to lash out with his fist. Although he hit her solidly in the face several times, it was a good many seconds before her fingers relaxed on his throat and she sagged to the bedsheets in unconsciousness.

Quinn caught his breath, then searched the woman's clothing. He discovered no personal effects of any kind, no wallet or money. Even the manufacturer's tags had been removed from the chambermaid's uniform. Reaching beneath her jaw, he peeled back the latex mask to reveal a young woman's face that bore the telltale, almost acromegalic, deformity characteristic of long-term steroid use.

Quinn picked up the room phone and dialed out. Bruckner's liaison asset picked up on the first ring, her voice as cool and manner as crisp as before. Quinn told the liaison about the chambermaid as he watched the woman sprawled on the bed moan and weakly move her head from side to side. The liaison asset said she would send some-one to deal with the woman.

A few minutes later there was another rap on the door. The deskman and the bellman were stand-ing in the hall.

"We regret the inconvenience," they said as they crossed toward the semiconscious woman who lay groaning on the bed. "Please accept the management's apologies."

The deskman took a hypodermic from inside his sport coat and plunged the blunt-nosed pneu-matic syringe into the woman's arm with prac-ticed skill, injecting the serum with a hiss of pressurized gas.

"A harmless though effective tranquilizer," he explained as the woman stopped moaning and again went completely limp. "With the added benefit of doubling as a truth drug."

The bellman by this time was unfolding a large black trash bag that he had taken from his pocket. The two hotel employees then stuffed the woman into the bag and dragged their burden toward the door.

"She is not one of our staff," the concierge told Quinn as they went out. "We will send up a bot-tle of champagne with the compliments of the house."

"Better make that a bottle of aspirin," Quinn said as he shut the door behind them. "Your room service has given me the mother of all headaches."

4

Quinn sipped his espresso and watched pigeons flutter around the Bernini fountain rising from the center of Piazzo Navona. He'd once heard the story that the Renaissance sculptor so detested the design of the church behind the fountain—and its architect—that he turned every face in the sculpture away from the building.

Bruckner's liaison arrived promptly for their meeting. At first blush, at least, her appearance fitted Quinn's initial assessment of her based on his phone conversation.

The dark business ensemble she wore was of a severe cut. It matched her long, angular face, which the lank, straight black hair she allowed to fall across her shoulders did little to soften.

Quinn watched Bruckner's agent speak to the maître d', then glance his way as the guy pointed to the table. A moment later she was seated across from him.

"There have been new developments," Ramsey said. "Since the demand to turn control of the Prometheus Net over to an as yet unknown force,

Koenig has been placed under round-the-clock surveillance. He has even consented to be implanted with a microchip that constantly monitors his vital signs."

"Sounds like the powers that be are taking no chances," Quinn concluded.

"They aren't," Ramsey returned.

"How about DiMarzio?" The Italian scientist had dropped out of sight the day before, according to the latest reports Quinn had received. "Have you succeeded in locating him?"

"Yes," Ramsey replied. "DiMarzio has been informed of our plans to interview him. At first he balked. However, he has consented to meet with us at his villa in Trastevere. The estate is a virtual fortress, equipped with the latest security devices. DiMarzio feels safe there, and only there. What are you laughing at?"

"I was thinking that the ancient Roman Caesars believed in tight security, too. In most cases it was their own mercenary troops who ultimately turned against them. In the end, few of them survived assassination attempts by their inner circle of sworn protectors."

THE LITTLE RADIANT pulled up to the gate of the villa. The guard eyed the Vietnamese compact car with hostility. No visitors were expected, and few in such cheaply made vehicles ever paid visits at all.

The guard ported his Beretta M3P bullpup autoshotgun at hip level as he approached the Radiant in open challenge. "What do you want?" he asked the driver.

The pretty young blonde smiled up at him, showing an even row of teeth. "Can you tell me if this is the road to Spoleto? We seem a little lost."

The guard began to say something in answer, but his outburst ended in a grunt of surprise and pain as the black-clad figure who had slid noiselessly behind him placed the muzzle of the silenced autopistol at the back of his head and fired a silenced hollow-nosed round into his brain.

The back of the guard's head burst apart in a bright shower of blood, and the man sagged to his knees on the graveled surface of the access road a moment later, then flopped forward onto his face.

The shooter dragged the dead man into the sentry booth and stashed him inside. At the same time another gunman jumped from the car. Moments later he returned and flashed them the thumbs-up, indicating he had just severed the villa's communications lines. Then he got back into the rear seat of the Radiant as the small car rolled up the long, sloping road toward the villa's main entrance.

Sagittarius One was right on schedule.

QUINN CLIMBED into the passenger seat of the Ferrari Velos. The engine of the sleek, powerful car roared to life as the Ferrari slid from the curb and entered the lane of Roman traffic. It was rush hour, and the roads were choked with vehicles maneuvering crazily everywhere in the Roman style.

"Don't let this gridlock fool you," Ramsey said as she honked her horn at a motorist in front of her who immediately signaled his annoyance but moved out of the way of the Ferrari just the same. "We won't be too long in this bottleneck, and then we're out of most of the traffic."

Quinn nodded. He wasn't concentrating on the traffic. He had other matters on his mind. "Bruckner told me you were Interpol. I logged into their data base before leaving the States. I was informed they had no record of you."

"I was formerly with a special branch," she returned. "As for my connection with Bruckner, like yourself, I'm a free-lancer who's currently affiliated with no organization. When this operation ends, my contract's completed."

"Have you worked with Bruckner long?" Quinn asked.

"No, not long," she replied, somewhat evasively Quinn thought. "At least not as long as you have. I understand you were affiliated with a top-secret counterterrorism program in the late nineties and early ten. Is that true?"

"Yes, that's right."

"But you dropped out suddenly," she continued. "Was there any reason in particular?"

"I'd rather not say," Quinn responded. "It might sound like a cliché, but that information happens to be classified."

"I understand," Ramsey answered matter-of-factly. She honked the horn, then sped out of the local traffic and shot ahead on the Rome-Salerno expressway, accelerating to the maximum without so much as a flinch on her expressionless face.

ALL THREE MERCENARIES in the Radiant donned black tactical face masks made of tissue-thin yet ultrahard synthetic material. The nonreflective material of their black action togs were crisscrossed with ALICE webbing from which various types of munitions were festooned.

Each Sagittarius striker carried a compact, sound-suppressor-equipped Spectre SMG. Jutting from the receiver of each Spectre was a staggered box magazine containing fifty hollow-nosed

9 mm rounds that could be ejected at a cycling rate of over eight hundred rounds per minute.

The high-capacity magazine of the Spectre gave the SMG the capability of unleashing devastating firepower at a sustained rate few weapons of its size and dimensions could deliver.

A white minivan was parked near the main entrance to DiMarzio's villa. It was crewed by two men, one in the cab, the other in the rear compartment. As the Radiant screamed up the drive at maximum speed, the van's side door trundled to one side, revealing the perforated black barrel of a pintle-mounted .50-caliber Browning machine gun bolted to the floor.

Before the Radiant had stopped completely, the two mercs in back were out of their seats, the sound-suppressed Spectre SMGs chattering in their fists. Low-trajectory automatic fire raked the van, killing the two protectors before they had a chance to fire their weapons at the strike team.

With the guards down, the Sagittarius snuff unit initiated the raid's terminal phase. While one of the three mercs blew the front doors with plastique button charges and raked the interior of the ground level with Spectre fire, the merc's companions whipped out harpoon guns and fired the line charges up at the balcony level of the villa.

The steel harpoons held fast against the balcony balustrade, and the two mercs scaled the side of the walls using the fiberglass lines they'd thrown. They found DiMarzio absorbed in his work in front of a portable computer. A moment later the female member of the team linked up with the two men on the upper story, having secured the ground level.

Classical music was playing on the sound system. The attack had been carried out so swiftly and so silently that the orbital propulsion dynamics specialist hadn't even been aware it had taken place.

"What is this?" DiMarzio cried out as he turned and saw the three dark-clad strikers now inside with him.

Springing forward, the point man placed a gloved hand over his mouth and held him immobilized in a powerful grip. DiMarzio struggled but couldn't get free.

At a nod from the strike leader one of the other two unshipped the stubby shape of a disposable plastic injector and jammed the blunt snout against the carotid artery on DiMarzio's pulsating throat.

There was a hiss of compressed gas as the Soman nerve agent was injected into his bloodstream. It began to take effect almost instantly. DiMarzio went rigid as his back arced against the powerful hands that held him, then went completely limp. The two male mercs then each grabbed one end of the kill and tossed DiMarzio's body out of the window of the upper story. The corpse hit the pool below with a splash and slowly sank just beneath the surface.

The Sagittarius strike crew extracted from the villa as quietly and swiftly as they had hit the target. Night had already fallen. Reentering the car, they removed their tactical face masks and, already on the move, the woman turned onto the highway, signaling via portable commo unit that the op had gone down as planned.

Inside the eighteen-wheel truck parked several miles away that served as their mobile command post, the merc seated at the console of computer banks issued Sagittarius One's next set of instructions. The team was to drive around Rome and await further orders.

The operative then deployed the robotized RPV, raising its launcher from a concealed compartment in the roof of the truck. Powered by small yet powerful solid propellant engines, the teardrop-fuselaged attack drone was airborne in seconds.

The remote-piloted vehicle's LLTV and TI camera gave immediate telemetry to the operative seated behind the console as it began a flight path toward the villa. The attack drone was heavily armed, and very dangerous.

5

The villa's iron gates swung ponderously in the warm, dry wind. The guardhouse appeared unoccupied. The air of abandonment gave Quinn an immediate sense of unease as the Ferrari turned off the highway and approached the estate.

"I'll go check it out," he told Ramsey, pulling the fully automatic Uzi machine pistol from the shoulder holster worn beneath his windbreaker.

The Uzi's staggered box magazine gave it a twenty-five-round capacity. Compensator-equipped, it was as stable as a handgun yet packed the wallop of a full-fledged SMG while offering the portability and concealability of a conventional large-frame handgun.

If Quinn expected Ramsey to remain in the vehicle, he was mistaken. She produced a Glock automatic from inside her handbag and cocked the slide, chambering a 9 mm PB round.

"I'll come with you," she said. Without waiting for Quinn's response she was out of the car.

"Looks like we're not the first visitors of the day," Quinn commented as he stared at the bloody remains sprawled on the floor of the sentry box.

Wary of ambush, they got back into the car and drove slowly toward the villa's main gate. The evidence of the Sagittarius strike was everywhere.

The shattered minivan stood with its windows blown out and a zigzag line of bullet holes stretching from front to rear fender. The dead driver's gun arm hung limply out the window, his head lolling to one side.

The man inside the rear of the van had been knocked back by the impact of the assault of massed Spectre fire. The barrel of the pintle-mounted Browning .50 was canted upward toward the roof of the van at a ninety-degree angle.

Weapons drawn, the two investigators entered the villa through its busted main doors, smelling the odors of high explosives and death. Inside, the corpses of the murdered guards lay sprawled here and there across the floor of the sunlit atrium. Splitting up, Quinn and Ramsey fanned out and took different paths on their search of the villa.

Following tradecraft, they would make certain the area was secure before proceeding, though Quinn for one suspected that the hit team had long since extracted from the scene. Quinn's guess proved correct. The only occupants of the villa beside themselves were the dead.

Quinn found DiMarzio sprawled facedown in his swimming pool. The underwater lights had been turned on, and the corpse floated with its limbs outstretched in the classic dead man's position.

The bloody strike zone was otherwise sterile. Quinn and Ramsey holstered their weapons. Ramsey was already communicating with Bruckner's UN-sanctioned covert task force command post via her palmtop phone. Utilizing signal-hopping filters for secure communication, the call would be immune to interception and decryption.

"The Rome police will be summoned after a brief delay," she told Quinn, signing off on her call. "We have only a few minutes to conduct a preliminary search before they arrive."

Hauling DiMarzio out of the water, Quinn proceeded to check the scientist's body. The pockets of DiMarzio's sodden clothing contained nothing of interest. Up in his room, the computer workstation that DiMarzio had been using at the time of his death was still turned on.

Quinn scrolled through the document on the screen, which displayed a scientific report Di-

Marzio had been working on. The computer records on the workstation yielded nothing, either.

The rest of the records stored in the computer's memory were entry-protected, but Quinn disengaged the bubble memory module from the machine's data slot. He would analyze it later. It might still yield a clue as to what, if anything, DiMarzio knew.

"I've got all I need," Quinn said to Ramsey. "How are you coming along?"

Ramsey was shooting the strike scene through a hand-held three-dimensional camcorder. She snapped the camcorder shut and dropped it into her purse.

Its removable data module had captured the entire scene in nonvolatile memory. The death zone could be analyzed in detail by holographic video later on.

"I'm through here," she told him. "Let's go."

SMALL YET POWERFUL rocket engines propelled the attack drone toward its programmed strike coordinates. The view screen in front of the merc codenamed Sagittarius flashed a position update as a shrill beep tone was emitted from the equipment. Keystroking in a series of commands, Sagittarius focused in on the Ferrari that was now rolling away from the villa, viewing it through the stand-off weapon's advanced sensorics.

Though its headlights were damped, invisible microwave laser light emitted by the RPV's sensor pod painted the car. Against the relative coolness of its surroundings, the heat signature of the car's engine and exhaust system caused it to stand out as clearly to the attack drone's thermal-imaging sensor head as though it were being viewed in broad daylight.

Seated at the control console in the mobile command center, Sagittarius smiled grimly. Pulling the gooseneck mike close to his thin, bloodless lips, he relayed the location of the Ferrari to the three mercs who'd taken down DiMarzio.

"DiMARZIO'S KILLERS must have beaten us to the villa by minutes," Ramsey said to Quinn.

"Don't be too hard on yourself," he advised her. "The opposition has been one jump ahead of us all along."

"Still, I—"

She never finished the sentence as the blinding flash of a proximity-fuzed airburst lit up the night. The Ferrari shuddered violently as the blast from the detonating submunition caved in its rear window, littering the back seat with granular debris.

Sixty feet overhead the remote-piloted vehicle fired another one of its rockets at the car. The airburst had shaken up the agents but hadn't scored a kill.

The second would. Sagittarius was confident.

Through the Ferrari's windshield Quinn saw something block out the stars in the cloudless night sky. It appeared to be too small to be a piloted helicraft, and Quinn immediately suspected the attack had been generated by an armed RPV.

Deafened by the blast, he could see Ramsey's lips move as she tried to speak to him from behind the wheel. Quinn fought to keep his concentration focused on the opposition's next move, indicating by hand signals that he couldn't hear her.

A brief flash signaled the launch of another warhead from the remote-piloted vehicle overhead. Ramsey jerked the wheel of the car, narrowly evading the second warhead strike by only a few feet. Blast waves slammed into the side of the vehicle, and it fishtailed to one side with the scream of tortured tire rubber, jumping the narrow curb and sideswiping the wall of one of the adjacent buildings.

Wrenching the wheel and flooring the gas pedal, Ramsey sent the car roaring down a nearby side street. High overhead, the RPV followed dog-gedly. On Sagittarius's remote command it switched from rocket bursts at the car to salvos of computer-controlled automatic fire from the gymbal-mounted .50-caliber machine gun in its nose assembly. A zigzag of heavy-caliber punctures slashed through the hood of the Ferrari as the MG opened up.

"Get out!" Quinn shouted as Ramsey stopped the car. Both passengers flung the doors open and jumped out, bolting for the protection of a pocket park just as the RPV fired another rocket warhead at the immobilized vehicle.

Scoring a direct hit, the round exploded. White-hot, semimolten shrapnel sheared through the fiberglass body of the car, igniting the high-octane fuel in the Ferrari's gas tank.

The explosion ripped the car to smithereens and reverberated through the narrow streets of the ancient Roman neighborhood, its blast strobing the surrounding wall with orange flickers.

Quinn raced across the street and grabbed the woman just as a line of automatic fire from the assault drone's .50-caliber gun walked its way across the cobblestones of the street behind her, throwing up a line of yellow sparks. Quinn shoved Ramsey forward into the shadows of an alley mouth as another salvo cut him off from the passage.

Flipping sideways, Quinn flattened against the side of a building, gripped the Uzi machine pistol in both hands and aimed at the dark shape circling overhead. Sighting the attack drone and tracking just ahead of its flight trajectory, Quinn squeezed off a burst of 9 mm Parabellums.

The fire was accurate. The steel jackets stitched the drone aircraft across the sensitive visionic pod situated in its nose assembly. In the mobile command center miles from the scene Sagittarius simultaneously saw his main video telemetry link blank out. He immediately switched to backup systems, but the drone's telemetry was spotty, broken up by earsplitting waves of rasping static.

Now operating without any guidance system to stabilize its flight, the RPV began to weave crazily in the night sky. Suddenly it tipped nose downward and began a power dive into the streets below. Moments later it crashed with a loud bang into the side of a building and immediately exploded into a cascade of white-hot sparks.

Sirens began to howl like banshees in the darkened streets of the city. Quinn looked down the narrow side alley he'd sent Ramsey into but could find no trace of her. Failing to locate her, he holstered his weapon and made his way into the darkness of a maze of alleylike passageways that led away from ground zero.

Quinn figured his female associate knew the rules of the game as well as he did. Tradecraft demanded that both of them extract from the hot action site and make contact later, if possible. For his own part, Quinn's priority one was to put as much distance between himself and the site of the abortive hit.

That, he was to discover quickly, was more easily said than done.

Informed by their command post unit of Quinn's last position, the Radiant with the three strikers who had hit DiMarzio on board had a fallback option of their own to pursue: swift termination of their quarry.

6

Quinn now assumed he was being hunted. By pros. The specialized hardware deployed in the strike meant that special operations personnel would almost certainly be deployed on the ground.

The name of the game of deadly hide-and-seek would be SLAM—a Search, Locate and Annihilate Mission.

Quinn mentally walked through tradecraft procedures the opposition would likely be putting into practice. The mercs would fan out, each taking a sector of the search zone. Street by street they would converge on the center of the zone until their quarry was caught in a multiple cross fire.

In these narrow passageways that turned and twisted and branched into one another without any apparent logic, it was a simple matter for a hunted man to become quickly and fatally disoriented. A single misstep could blow the whole game, a turn of a corner at the wrong moment could bring Quinn into firing range of a hostile gun.

Control of the killing ground was the all-important objective. The brass ring would go to whichever side was capable of best navigating through the labyrinth of these meandering Roman alleys.

WITH THE ATTACK DRONE now out of commission, the three Sagittarius strikers were on their own. Deploying silently through the maze of twisting streets, the wolf pack was on the hunt, on the attack, in their element. Having donned night-vision goggles to give them added night-seeing capability, the mercenary snuff detail would pose double the trouble.

Lucking out quickly, one member of the strike trio picked up Quinn near a statue in a shadowy cul-de-sac at the intersection of three narrow alleys. Quarry limned in green raster light, framed in the center of the white target acquisition reticle, the merc raised his SMG for a put-away burst.

He had his target in the killbox. A quick, silenced burst would send him straight to hell.

Nomad heard the faint rustle of cloth behind him. He spun around, sighted the lethal shadow profile of the hunter-killer and darted sideways just as a burst of sound-suppressed Spectre fire thudded into the base of the statue.

Fisting his SMG in a two-handed grip, Nomad threw his outstretched arms across the hood of the car behind which he crouched and sighted on the dark alley mouth from where the fire had come ripping. But the striker had already vanished into the shadows.

Quinn blinked hard as he swept his eyes back and forth but still failed to acquire a target. The striker was gone.

Anticipating the nameless terminators stalking him from the shadows to strike again soon, Quinn knew it would be dangerous to stay where he was. So he broke from cover and ran across the yawning expanse of the cul-de-sac toward an alley to one side of the dark passageway from which the merc had struck.

Cloaked in shadows, the merc sighted his SMG on the running man and sent the bolt hammering on a chambered bullet. A deadly salvo of 9 mm hornets buzzed at Quinn's heels. The rotoring PBs punched into the cobblestone street behind him as he beelined for cover.

Gaining the alley's mouth one step ahead of the lancing PBs that tore chips of mortar from the building wall, Quinn whipped his own hardware into firing position and instantly brought the Uzi into play.

From a half crouch, with the Uzi studded on full-burst fire, Nomad triggered a storm of answering steel in his antagonist's direction.

The NVG-equipped terminator sprinted back into the cul-de-sac and ducked for cover of a van parked nearby, as quick on his feet as Nomad was. From this secure position he raised his weapon for an instant replay of lethal hellfire, but Nomad was nowhere to be seen.

The striker was puzzled as he scanned the perimeter through the green visual field of the NVGs. Where the hell had he gone?

Waiting a few pulse beats, the merc walked on a stealthy crouch down the line of parked cars, then popped up several feet from his last position. The SMG in his fist tracked the area in sweeping arcs while he scanned the covert firezone through his night-seeing goggles.

There was still no sign of his quarry.

The merc smiled. Quinn might run, but he couldn't hide. Not for long. The merc had his quarry spooked. Endgame was near, he sensed.

Then he saw the flicker of movement just within the mouth of one of the narrow alleys that fed into the pocket square. Bingo, the merc thought. He'd grown up in the streets of Rome and knew that this particular alley was blind.

The merc was up from cover a pulse beat later, sprinting across the small square. When he reached the alley mouth, he threw suppressing fire into it, using his NVGs to pierce through the darkness within. Detecting no sign of movement, the merc loaded a fresh clip into the Spectre, then duckwalked into the alley, cautiously panning his head from side to side.

Though the alley was completely dark, the NVGs made the killzone appear as bright as high noon. Quinn would have a hard time drawing an accurate bead on him, whereas the striker's vision was excellent. He had the edge, and he would use it to shut his opponent out.

Had the merc noticed the empty refrigerator carton lying discarded against a wall, perhaps he would have won the game, after all.

Inside the box, his Uzi fisted and ready, Quinn crouched. He heard the muffled slap of his hunter's boot soles against the worn cobbles as he slid past in the shadows.

Quinn counted a beat, then sprang from the box, his SMG steady in a double-fisted sharpshooter's grip. The striker spun around fast just as Nomad brought his hardware into violent play. The black figure on his green visual field already had the drop on him. Though he knew he was a dead man, the striker triggered a hip-level Spectre burst just as Quinn's gun sounded its chattering knell.

A shining finger of Uzi Parabellums reached out and touched the one-upped merc in the center of his chest, shattering the breastbone and collarbone and penetrating beyond to shear through heart and lung tissue that emerged from a gaping exit wound in the striker's back in a splattering crimson plume.

The striker's eyes widened beneath the twin light-amplification tubes of his NVG as death's finger moved on, vaporizing his throat into a fine, bloody mist. The merc took a halting step forward and tried to lift his weapon while a flicker of life and strength still remained in his body.

But the Spectre suddenly weighed a thousand pounds. It was the heaviest thing in the universe. With each second that passed, the weight of the SMG increased until he could no longer hold on to it at all.

The Spectre dropped from his hand as he pitched forward onto his face, then rolled sideways to wind up with arms outstretched and blood draining from the ragged holes the slugs had augered in his body.

Quinn tore the NVGs from the dead merc's head. His gaze came to rest on the sightless eyes, which bulged in death. Cruelty was etched into the features of the covert terminator. Even dead, the face had the hard look of a professional thug.

After cleaning them of blood on the dead merc's clothes, Quinn strapped the NVGs around his own neck and pulled the Starlite goggles over his face. The darkness of the shadowy street instantly dissolved, replaced by the spectral green glow of the light-amplification device's viewing field, confirming that the NVGs were functional.

Quinn rifled quickly through the pockets of the downed merc's clothing. As he had expected, the search yielded no evidence concerning the dead field asset's identity, mission, command center location or operation manager.

Quinn couldn't find a passport or a wallet, either. There wasn't even a single scrap of evidence to confirm or deny the existence of the merc.

Quinn holstered his Uzi machine pistol and checked the clip of the Spectre SMG captured from the opposition. The compact yet lethal subgun still had twenty-five rounds of 9 mm PB ammunition left in its high-capacity magazine. In addition to the clip in the Spectre's receiver, the downed covert striker carried spare clips in the pockets of his windbreaker.

Quinn holstered the Uzi, now choosing to port the Spectre because of its greater firepower and magazine capacity. He removed the half-empty clip, pocketed it and snapped a full clip of hollow-nosed PBs into the Spectre. Then Quinn dragged the body into the shadows and stuffed it inside the same refrigerator carton in which he'd taken cover.

With one merc down the rules of the game had shifted in Quinn's favor. His posture could now shift from evasion to attack. From kill to counterkill.

QUINN WAITED in the shadows, crouched behind a low wall of ancient masonry that surrounded a small garden, peering through the grille of a wrought-iron gate.

The other two members of the covert death squad now came suddenly into view. They were rolling down the street in the Radiant, transmission in low gear, headlights damped.

The driver must have spotted the telltale pockmarks of recent autofire on the ancient brick walls of a nearby building. The Radiant stopped and the two commandos broke silently through each of the Radiant's doors.

Watching through NVGs, Nomad smiled grimly. Sighting his commandeered SMG, he squeezed off a Parabellum burst that dropped the taller one of the hostile ground assets a few feet from the Radiant.

The lone surviving merc whirled, snapped off a sound-suppressed autoburst on the fly from the Spectre he ported and made tracks around the corner of a nearby alley, too fast for Quinn to draw an accurate bead.

Up from cover, Quinn charged after the fleeing operative, chasing the small, nimble man down the dark, twisting passageways that were taking them toward the Colosseum area. Nomad soon caught up with his quarry near the gates of the Forum of the Caesars.

The cornered operative whirled and snapped an autoburst at Nomad, then vaulted the high iron fence surrounding the Forum and was quickly lost within the ancient ruins.

Nomad scaled the fence and was inside the Forum right behind the running man, scrambling for cover as a hail of sustained PB autofire rotored his way from deeper inside the rubble-littered zone of broken columns, shattered arches and crumbling walls.

In the open again moments after the firing ceased, Nomad cautiously negotiated the broken terrain. Although his night-seeing goggles provided excellent visibility, he was aware that the merc shooter could be lurking anywhere within the maze of ruined masonry, waiting to blow him away, and that the merc, too, was NVG-equipped.

Surrounded by remnants of a vanished civilization, Quinn felt as though he had stepped backward in time into another age in which savage gladiatorial combat had been practiced as a blood sport. Stalking his prey, he felt he was enacting a timeless drama, as though the ancient Roman gods were watching expectantly from above with fiery red eyes.

The merc was waiting in ambush behind the Arch of Titus. As Quinn came abreast of one of the arch's supports, the merc stepped from hiding and opened up with a long, hip-level burst of SMG steel.

Quinn caught sight of the operative as he brought his hardware into play, and fast legwork allowed him to dodge the tracking line of deadly nines and dive behind the cover of a nearby wall section, but not before his NVGs sustained a random hit that knocked them out of commission.

With Quinn's vision now impaired, the night-scope had instantly turned from an asset into a serious liability. Ripping the useless image-intensification device from his head, Nomad flung down the NVGs as he hunkered behind the wall, scenting the coolness of earth, feeling the near-ness of death.

Afterimages floated across Quinn's eyes, a re-sult of the sudden transition from NVGs to unaided sight. Because his vision hadn't had time to adjust to the darkness, he knew he would be al-most completely blind for the next few seconds. He crouched in the shadows and listened as the visual impairment slowly began to fade and his night vision returned.

Suddenly Quinn felt something prod the back of his head.

"Stand up, cowboy," the merc hissed.

Quinn rose to his feet. The seconds of blind-ness and disorientation had been enough to allow his adversary to creep up on his position and get the drop on him. As he stood, the merc roughly grabbed the Spectre from Quinn's hand and tossed it into the shadows.

The smaller man smiled as he stepped away from Quinn, keeping the blunt-ended snout of the Spectre SMG pointed at his face. The twin camera lenses of the NVGs he wore glowed with an eerie inner light. He raised the Spectre to shoulder height and sighted along the barrel at the side of Quinn's head.

"You lose," he said with a smile.

Then a gunshot cracked, and Nomad saw the merc stagger forward as if he had just been kicked in the small of the back. There was no one behind him, though, but the sudden spout of red that glittered from the center of his chest meant that the merc had been struck from behind by a well-aimed round.

As the mortally wounded man sagged to the rubble-strewn earth, Nomad swept the area with his eyes and saw the figure standing by the railing of the overlook above the ruins, silhouetted against the faint glow that the streetlights of downtown Rome imparted to the night sky.

It was Ramsey, a weapon in her hand.

Quinn stooped and pulled the NVGs and black nylon watch cap from the cammied face of the terminated striker, realizing with a start that the attacker was a woman.

A woman with beautiful blond hair.

7

The interactive hologram video shot by Ramsey revealed the execution scene in full detail. Quinn and she were able to walk their way around the killing zone, examining the three-dimensional images of the body found at the pool. The Rome safe house supplied by the Interpol-coordinated intelligence coalition was fully equipped with the latest analysis equipment.

There was a great deal of information to digest. The clock was ticking toward the date of the Prometheus network's activation and Koenig's speech before the United Nations General Assembly in New York.

Quinn had succeeded in breaking the encryption cipher used to access the protected documents stored in DiMarzio's computer memory. They appeared to be technical documents connected with his research for the international consortium that had constructed the Prometheus satellite network launch system.

DiMarzio's specialty was in the field of advanced software design, and the documents appeared to offer no clue as to why he, like the other Prometheus technicians, had been singled out for termination.

Ramsey switched off the interactive video, and the hologram faded slowly from view. "That wraps it up for me," she told him.

Seated at the computer, Quinn turned in the swivel chair. Ramsey was watching him intently, a half smile on her face.

"I'm for the shower, Quinn," she said a moment later, turning to go. "Good night."

Quinn nodded and turned back to the computer. With an operative like her there was no point in attempting to read anything into what might otherwise be a meaningful look. That was just as well.

The risks of fraternizing while on an assignment were far too great to permit emotion to intrude on a professional relationship. Quinn read the lady as a pro and didn't give her lingering glance another thought. Moments later he heard the hiss of the shower in the adjoining bathroom of the safe house. Absorbed in his work at the computer, Quinn lost track of time. Hours passed before he, too, turned in on a cot set against the wall.

Just before dawn Quinn was awakened by the presence of someone in the room. He drew the .38-caliber H&K pistol he'd hidden beneath his pillow and aimed it at the figure.

"You don't need that," Ramsey whispered, pushing aside the gun as she slid in beside Quinn.

IN A PLACE KNOWN only as Castle the lights never went out. The large, sterile chamber in which the Council convened was dominated by a low-slung conference table.

Around the conference table sat a group of men. They were screening a recent address by an individual many hailed as the greatest visionary to have come out of Germany in the past two hundred years.

Wilhelm Koenig stood before the symbol of his peace party, the design of interlocking sevens that symbolized the unity of the new world order of the twenty-first century.

Some claimed that this design was too reminiscent of the Nazi swastika. Koenig's response was that even the swastika was an ancient symbol of good fortune before Hitler had corrupted its meaning forever.

Koenig's weathered face bore the lines of the adversity he had suffered in his life. Every schoolchild on the planet knew the story of Koenig's crusade to make his dream of a new millennium a reality for the human race.

Alpha's holographic telepresence facsimile appeared as the screen blanked out. The three-dimensional hologram of Alpha was larger than life, appearing to stand eight feet in height.

There was no way of knowing if the holofax of Alpha depicted their leader's true image, or if it were a completely computer-generated simulation. There was also no way of being sure of where exactly the holofax was being transmitted from.

Alpha could be anywhere on earth. He could just as easily be here in Castle, perhaps in a small room adjacent to the Council itself.

"Aries. Your report."

Alpha's electronically altered voice was as smooth as jet but as cold as steel. Every member of the Council knew that he was capable of wasting them all without an eye blink.

The one known as Aries rose from his seat and began his briefing. Those in the room had no identities, their only denominations being the constellations of the zodiac from which they took their names and to which their functions were ascribed.

Aries was the ram and responsible for technological matters, including sabotage and disruption.

"The Prometheus computer has been invaded successfully," Aries declared. "The viral codes have already corrupted data beyond all hope of salvage. My unit anticipates no impediments."

"Thank you, Aries. Sagittarius, your report."

The second speaker rose and cleared his throat. He was an urbane-looking man with graying temples and a deep voice. Sagittarius, the archer, was responsible for carrying out the strikes in Rome.

"The American agent sent by the intelligence coalition is being tracked," Sagittarius reported. "When he is located again, he'll be dealt with."

Silence hung in the air as heavy as a leaden shroud as the second speaker concluded his report.

Sagittarius didn't sit. Instead he continued to stand. Alpha hadn't yet given Sagittarius permission to do anything else.

"You were issued a termination directive, Sagittarius," the electronic voice of Alpha said softly, almost innocently, like the voice of a child. "Why was it not carried out?"

"It, I mean, the coalition's operative code-named Nomad—he escaped the hunters."

Sagittarius's voice betrayed the speaker's profound anxiousness. He didn't dare risk a glance at those sitting around the table. Sagittarius knew the other members of the Council silently mocked him, waited like jackals for him to stumble and fall. But Sagittarius wouldn't.

"Don't worry," he went on, trying but failing to sound more confident. "I assure you, Alpha, it won't happen again. Nomad will be dealt with."

Alpha's voice seemed especially soft when he next spoke. Most of the members present in the room thought they detected a slight undertone of menace this time, however.

"You are quiet correct, Sagittarius," Alpha said. "It will not happen again." He paused a beat while Sagittarius waited, a cold sweat beading his forehead. "Your presence will not be required for the rest of the Council's meeting. You may go, Sagittarius."

"But—" Sagittarius stammered.

"You may *go,*" Alpha interrupted softly.

Sagittarius turned and walked with nervous quickness toward the doorway located some distance from the table. He only got halfway there.

Overhead, a panel in the ceiling slid open on silent runners. A shaft of green laser light struck Sagittarius squarely between the shoulder blades.

Arms outstretched, Sagittarius toppled forward. In the center of his back there was now a smoking hole. The nauseating stench of ozone and cauterized flesh suddenly filled the Council chamber.

The section of the floor on which the smoldering corpse of Sagittarius was sprawled began to descend soundlessly, taking Sagittarius with it into the depths of Castle.

Even before the floor panel slid quietly back into place, disposal equipment was already grinding up the remains of the Council member who had failed to carry out his assigned directive.

"We will now proceed to other business," Alpha's strange velveteen voice echoed softly through the Council room. "Capricorn and Virgo. Your reports."

QUINN WAS RUNNING through his morning exercise routine of t'ai chi ch'uan exercises. The slow, graceful movements had been developed as an adjunct to the martial arts.

After a few minutes of preliminary exercises, Quinn found himself slipping into another realm of consciousness. He switched to lightning-fast hwa rang do movements, sparring with an opponent in his mind as he went through the *kata* of the ancient fighting technique that blended martial arts with hard combat training.

"Very good," he heard Ramsey's voice say as he assumed a pigeon-toed stance and finally allowed himself to relax. "Your form is excellent."

"You've been watching me," he responded.

"Yes, I have," Ramsey told him. "I hope you don't mind."

"Not at all."

She offered him a cup of steaming coffee, saying nothing about what had happened the night before, acting as if nothing whatever had taken place between them. Quinn accepted the steaming cup and drank, realizing that, in fact, their encounter was a nonstarter.

Ramsey had seen fit to use his body for her own selfish reasons, and he had taken pleasure from hers in return. It had been an even trade for both of them.

Just then the videophone beeped. It was Bruckner. Over the secure communications link Bruckner told Quinn and Ramsey both that the mercs who had attacked them in Rome couldn't be traced to any source.

Their identities were clean.

No record existed of them.

"There is now conclusive proof that a computer virus or viruses have infected the Prometheus program," Bruckner went on. "It's still preliminary, but the tech boys figure it's probably more than one kind. We've got the CERT team—the computer emergency response team—in there right now going over the system with a fine-tooth comb. So far, though, the CERT team hasn't even scratched the surface."

"How about Koenig's upcoming UN address?" Quinn asked. "Can it be changed?"

"Negative," Bruckner replied, shaking his head. "Koenig won't stand for it. The UN won't stand for it. The President of the United States won't stand for it. Any change in timing and the entire project could be jeopardized. The speech is still on, no matter what."

"Is Koenig in protective custody?" Ramsey asked.

"Yes, he is," Bruckner told her. "Nothing gets in or out of the net surrounding him without being put through the tightest security screening you ever saw."

Unfortunately, Quinn thought, that in itself didn't mean much. No one had to remind Quinn or Ramsey that some of the remaining Prometheus scientists, including DiMarzio, had met their ends despite stringent security measures.

Quinn and Ramsey signed off. After Quinn had a postworkout shower, they left the safehouse and headed out to the airport. Their next stop from Ciampino was to be Van Sicklen in Brussels, one of the few Prometheus techs still alive.

8

Dr. Gropius Van Sicklen was a portly man of middle years with a Vandyke beard and a large, wedgelike nose. Were it not for the gray jogging suit and track shoes he wore on his regular morning jog, he might have just stepped out of a painting by Rembrandt or Vermeer.

The internationally renowned expert on space-based lasers enjoyed his daily runs around his favorite park in the old quarter of the city. Years of diligent exercise had kept his physique trim and his mind sharp. Van Sicklen believed that a slack body made for a slack mind, and the latter was nothing that a man in his line of work could tolerate.

Since completing work on Prometheus's microwave laser energy transfer system, Van Sicklen had been feeling oddly depressed. His rigorous exercise regimen was even more important to him now, he felt. Only with the exhilaration of running could he fend off the depression that lurked like a dark shadow in the corners of his mind.

Van Sicklen attributed these feelings of unease to the dual-use aspect of the microwave technology. He had issued numerous warnings as to the dangers inherent in the highly active microwave energy waveforms that beamed the collected solar energy to earth-based receiving stations.

These microwaves were also capable of punching great holes in the atmosphere's ozone layer, he had stated. If control of the Prometheus Net fell into the wrong hands, disaster might ensue. Instead of heeding his warning, however, the project's chief technician had censured Van Sicklen.

Wilhelm Koenig was a man with a vision, and like many visionaries before him, intolerant of anyone who challenged his vision or anything that might hinder its realization. In the end Van Sicklen's warnings had been brushed aside and work on Prometheus had gone ahead as planned.

Having completed his jog, Van Sicklen got into his car and drove home. He showered and read the morning papers while he watched the latest news reports on the multiple video screens of the media center occupying most of the south wall of his study.

There was a sudden knock on the door. His housekeeper, Mrs. Haagan, came into the study a few minutes later, carrying a pile of neatly folded clothing.

"Your costume is all ready," she told Van Sicklen with a smile that made the corners of her blue eyes crinkle merrily. "I've made a few special changes this year, sir."

Van Sicklen smiled back at his housekeeper. "Good," he told her. "I know you've done a marvelous job." Mrs. Haagen had served him for many years, and he trusted her judgment implicitly when it came to all matters domestic.

Minutes later, having blanked off the giant high-definition video screen that delivered the morning news, Van Sicklen put on the clothes that Mrs. Haagen had laid out for him on one of the study's overstuffed easy chairs. Standing in front of a full-length mirror, he appraised his housekeeper's handiwork with a critical eye.

Mrs. Haagen had done well, Van Sicklen saw immediately. The Jester suit was cleanly pressed, and small rips made last year had been expertly mended.

When the time came, in a few more hours, he would apply the garish white greasepaint to his face and don the fright wig of carrot-colored hair upon which would perch the long conical hat with a pom-pom on its end.

Today marked the start of the annual Festival of the Cats, the Belgian Kattestoet. Van Sicklen was once again to take pride of place as the festival's Jester.

As Jester, his role would be to fling stuffed cats from the balcony of the city hall building that stood in the center of Brussels. Originating in nearby Ieper, the Kattestoet had grown in popularity until the huge crowds it attracted each year had made Brussels a more natural site.

In assuming the role, Van Sicklen was carrying on a tradition that had been passed down from father to son for several generations.

The grim-faced men from Interpol had paid him a visit, and Van Sicklen was well aware of the danger he faced from unknown threats. He didn't fully understand the nature of these threats but had little doubt they were real. The strange deaths of his fellow Prometheus technicians had convinced him of this beyond all shadow of a doubt.

It had taken a great deal of explaining to the law-enforcement personnel, but finally Van Sicklen had made them understand that the role of Jester of the Festival of the Cats was one which he couldn't possibly turn down. This was no frivolous carousing, the scientist had insisted, but a solemn duty that he was set on carrying out, come what may. To refuse to act as Jester would be to disgrace his family's good name and betray an ancient trust.

"How do I look?" he asked Mrs. Haagan, who had just come back into the study and stood looking at him with a broad smile on her matronly features. "Do I not make a fine Jester?"

"You certainly do, Doctor," she replied, nodding vigorously. "But I fear that those men outside don't appreciate the importance of your role in the festival."

"Well, I'm afraid they are a different breed," Van Sicklen said. He glanced out the window of the study and saw two of the men in dark business suits and sunglasses who had surrounded his house for the past week.

My protectors, he thought to himself, shaking his head in dismay. There was no way that Van Sicklen could rid himself of the policemen, but there was also no way the police could prevent him from attending the festival as Jester. Van Sicklen supposed they would simply both have to learn to live with each other, at least for a few hours more. He would make the best of things, though, he thought as he turned to Mrs. Haagen again. "Why don't you offer our caretakers some of that good hot American coffee you've just made?" he asked.

"Very well, sir," Mrs. Haagen responded as she left the room with a sigh, making a sour face at the policemen outside. Minutes later Dr. Van Sicklen saw his housekeeper carrying steaming mugs on a silver tray out to them. With a laugh he turned back to admiring his Jester's suit in the full-length mirror.

"YOU'VE JUST MISSED THEM," Mrs. Haagen told Quinn and Ramsey as they arrived at the Prometheus scientist's house. "My employer and the policemen left just a short while ago. For the cat festival, you know."

Quinn looked around. The house was impeccably kept, and every surface gleamed. The place seemed to radiate an atmosphere of comfort and care and had a peculiar fresh scent created by regular cleaning and the application of fine wax on handcrafted hardwood furniture.

"One of the policemen who escorted Dr. Van Sicklen left something for you," Mrs. Haagen went on, then produced a small plastic cube with a blue push button on its top. It was a standard telefax memo cube. She handed it to Quinn, then left the room, telling them on her way out to call her if they needed anything.

"I'm agent Broswith," the telefax said as Quinn played it in Van Sicklen's media center. "My team has the doctor well in hand. You may interview the doctor after he's completed his function as Jester."

The telefax faded, and the cube emitted a final beep tone, signifying the end of the prerecorded memo. Just then Mrs. Haagen appeared with a silver tray on which was a ceramic server and two cups.

"You'll at least stay for coffee," she said to them, smiling brightly. "Dr. Van Sicklen asked me to be sure to make you feel at home in his absence."

Quinn thanked the housekeeper and reached for one of the Delft cups. If the Prometheus technician was intent on playing the Jester today, there was no point in rushing. He and Ramsey sipped the coffee and enjoyed some of Mrs. Haagen's fresh-baked pastries that had just come out of her oven.

Having gone through the motions of gracious visitors, Quinn and Ramsey left Van Sicklen's house and climbed back into the Audi that they had driven there from the airport to begin a trip along the highway into the center of town.

As they drove away, Mrs. Haagen removed a small black telecommunication device from beneath her apron and turned it on. Her face was no longer smiling, and her blue eyes no longer radiated a trace of their former warmth.

"This is Scorpio Two. Subjects have just left," she said into the commo unit in a voice that had completely lost every shred of its former graciousness. "Scorpio One—prepare to intercept and terminate."

9

Quinn and Ramsey drove along the modern highway complex that ribboned toward the city center. Most of the cars they passed bore indications
that their passengers were on their way to the festival.

Adults and children alike wore cat costumes,
and the highway was much more congested with
traffic than was normal, even for a Sunday afternoon in late spring.

Quinn's mind began drifting from the immediate assignment toward thoughts about the woman
sitting beside him. From what he'd seen, Quinn
had no doubt she was a competent professional,
cool and dependable under fire.

She had exhibited many of these same attri-
butes in her lovemaking, too, but so far she had
said nothing about what had gone down at the
Rome safe house, almost as if she had already
forgotten it as she might any other purely functional biological process. Quinn didn't take of-
fense at this fact, and indeed he was grateful for it.

He had long since put aside any considerations of male ego when it came to the business of covert operations. In fact, had he felt otherwise or sensed that Ramsey did he would have immediately phoned Bruckner and informed him he was bowing out of the mission.

Feelings of any kind were dangerous to an asset on the ground. They got in the way. In the covert firezone they might well have fatal consequences for all parties concerned.

Quinn sensed, however, that there was a lot more to Bruckner's liaison asset than met the eye. He wondered about her personal history but knew better than to ask her outright. What seductions had she practiced for her paymasters in the past? Where had Bruckner recruited her from? Was she CIA, KGB, Mossad, Mukhabarat or a free-lancer like himself?

Quinn's thoughts soon turned back to the business at hand as Ramsey swung the Audi off the highway and approached the center of the city. The festival was already beginning to take off, he could see. The route that the parade of giant cat floats and feline-costumed marchers would take had been cordoned off to automobile traffic, and spectators were already jockeying for positions along the route.

"Might as well go the rest of the way on foot," Quinn told Ramsey as they exited the Audi and merged with the huge crowd of pedestrians. "There are still a couple of hours to go until we can meet with Van Sicklen, and we're probably lucky to have found parking at all."

Hawkers had set up stalls and were selling gaudy wares of all kinds, with special emphasis on souvenirs with a feline theme. Quinn stepped up to one of the stalls, which was festooned with every conceivable trinket and geegaw from small, artfully made cat dolls to wristwatches with cat faces.

"What do you know about this festival?" he asked Ramsey as he motioned to the merchant that he didn't want to buy a hat that sported a cat's bewhiskered face on its brim.

"It was originally begun in the Middle Ages to guard the populace of Ieper against the plague," Ramsey answered. "The conventional wisdom of the time held that cats were evil, creatures to be loathed and feared. As such, they were considered responsible for all manner of diseases and misfortunes that afflicted mankind."

As Quinn listened, he took out a noncarcinogenic filter cigarette, thumbed off its self-igniting cap and deeply inhaled the rich menthol smoke. His eye was caught by a couple leading their two children. All four were dressed in color-coordinated cat costumes.

"At first," Ramsey continued, speaking precisely as if reading from a prepared text, "actual cats were hurled from the windows of a high belfry. The barbaric custom was eventually discontinued when it was discovered that cats ate the rats that carried the germs causing bubonic plague. But in 1938 the custom of throwing cats from a belfry was revived—this time using stuffed cat dolls in place of the live cats of the previous era."

"And these are the cats the Jester throws down to the onlookers in the square at the conclusion of the parade?"

"That's correct," Ramsey said to Quinn.

Soon the parade was in full swing. Standing on the sidelines, Quinn and Ramsey watched the showy floats featuring enormous papier-mâché felines glide past them to the cheering of thousands of onlookers.

The floats rivaled anything he had seen in the States, even at Mardi Gras in New Orleans, and although the crowd was much more subdued than a Mardi Gras crowd, the Belgians seemed as enthusiastic as they came, at least as far as parades went.

While Quinn and Ramsey watched the parade floats, other members of the crowd were watching them. One hundred fifty miles above the earth, in a low geosynchronous orbit, a spy satellite had been tracking their car ever since their arrival in Brussels.

The satellite had provided those monitoring its telemetry with the precise location of the UN-mandated investigators tracking down the surviving Prometheus personnel. Now that the techint had been confirmed and visual contact had been established by humint assets on the ground, the intelsat was shifted to another orbit, tasked with monitoring other targets.

The assets on the ground grasped the weapons concealed in holsters worn beneath their cat costumes. For the present their orders were to follow but not to initiate direct contact. They would continue to do so until they received orders to the contrary.

Then they would do what they had been trained to do: kill.

IN HIS JESTER'S SUIT, Dr. Van Sicklen inspected the bin containing the ceremonial cat dolls that he would fling down to the waiting crowds in only a little while. The stuffed cats were custom-made in

Hong Kong to the festival committee's precise specifications.

Van Sicklen picked up one of the toy cats and noted its rhinestone eyes, fiberglass whiskers and tawny nylon fur. He flipped the cat back into the bin among dozens of others just like it.

"Quite a nice batch this year," the festival committee's chairman, Max Gilparzer, said to him. "We've switched to a new factory. They do excellent work."

"Yes, you're right," Van Sicklen answered. "Well, it's about time I put on my Jester makeup," he added.

Van Sicklen turned and walked into the dressing room that had been prepared for him. It was the building janitor's office, which had been outfitted with an old dressing table.

As Van Sicklen began applying his makeup, he heard a small rustling sound from somewhere behind him. Turning, he saw a man wearing green coveralls step from behind the concealment of a row of tall filing cabinets. The man smiled, and Van Sicklen recognized him at once. He was the building's janitor.

"What are you doing here?" Van Sicklen demanded, unable to tear his eyes from the automatic pistol that the newcomer gripped in his hand, a pistol that bore the long cylinder of a sound-suppression device jutting from its business end. "What is the meaning of this?"

The janitor's gun spoke for him, coughing again and again as it spit three hollow-nosed 9 mm rounds in quick succession into his face.

Van Sicklen was catapulted back in his chair by the impact of the consecutively fired rounds. Blood burst from the pulverized cheeks and shattered jaw, streaming in a dark gush down the colorful Jester suit. After a moment, the corpse sagged forward and thudded to the floor, crimson fluid pooling around the smashed-in head.

After holstering his weapon, the janitor dragged Van Sicklen to the concealment of the filing cabinets, cleaned up the blood and then retrieved the spent shell casings from the trio of slugs.

Once he had retrieved the brass, the janitor unzipped his green coveralls. Beneath them he was wearing a Jester suit identical in every detail to the one Van Sicklen was wearing. Then, taking the seat in front of the mirror, he began to apply heavy theatrical greasepaint to his face, followed by the long red plastic nose, the fright wig of carrot-red hair and the floppy Jester hat.

There was a rap on the door, and the committee chairman poked his head into the room. "Are you ready?" Gilparzer asked.

The man in the Jester suit half turned and waved at the chairman. "Five minutes," he said as he coughed into his hand, making his voice come out as a muffled rasp.

"Very good. I'll inform the others," the chairman said as he closed the door.

QUINN SIPPED from a plastic cup full of draft beer as he watched a gaudily painted thirty-foot-high papier-mâché cat roll by on hidden wheels. Scantily clad girls rode its back and tail, waving at the passersby and throwing small cat dolls into the crowd. The Kattestoet was now in full swing.

Noisy, bustling crowds lined the path of the parade, waving and clapping and whistling. Many in the crowd were made up to look like cats in addition to wearing cat costumes, and a cat blimp passed overhead with a banner in tow advertising a local department store.

"It's almost time for the Jester to appear," Ramsey said as she checked her watch. "Let's get up closer to the city hall building."

They made their way to the edge of the police barricades set up to hold the crowds back from the city hall's front. Just then the Jester made his appearance on the balcony high above them, and the crowd let out a sudden, frantic scream.

10

The Jester waved to the crowd as he stepped out onto the balcony. Below him the assemblage shouted their eagerness to receive the traditional cat dolls that the Jester threw down. Picking the first of many toy cats from the bin with a flourish, the Jester hurled his first offering into the anxious crowd waiting below. As it tumbled end over end through space, the wind caught the doll and it began to drift off course. Moments later it dropped into a mass of outstretched hands.

The crowd gave out a cheer as a man to Quinn's right caught the first cat thrown by the Jester, holding it up in one hand in a gesture of victory while letting out a joyous whoop. It was considered good luck to catch the first cat that the Jester tossed.

"The wind sure can make a difference in who gets a cat," Quinn observed aloud to Ramsey as they watched the Jester snatch up a second cat doll and prepare to hurl it into the crowd.

It, too, was picked up by the gusting winds and wound up sailing several feet from the trajectory it would be expected to follow in less turbulent air.

Now the Jester was beginning to hurl the stuffed felines faster and faster. The crowd, sensing that the supply of cat dolls would soon dwindle down to nothing, was becoming rowdier and rowdier by the minute. Although the Belgians were showing restraint, people were beginning to push and shove a little in their eagerness to catch the last few cat dolls hurled down by the Jester.

Finally the Jester picked up a cat and, by hand gestures, communicated to the crowd that this was the last of his dolls to be distributed at this year's festival. Quinn motioned to Ramsey to get ready to enter the city hall building for their too-long-delayed interview with Van Sicklen now that his part in the festival was coming to an end.

Unlike with his other tosses, however, the Jester now seemed to be looking directly at Quinn as he raised the doll high over his head and hurled it downward. As the doll fell, Quinn realized something was wrong. Dangerously wrong. The doll wasn't behaving the same way the others had behaved.

In a sudden flash of comprehension he realized what that discrepancy was. The wind wasn't changing the direction of this doll, and unlike the other dolls thrown, it was plummeting straight toward them, as an object too heavy to be affected by the wind would behave. As an object stuffed with a high-explosive charge and a proximity-fuzed detonator might.

Quinn reached out to Ramsey and shouted a warning to her, knowing full well there wasn't enough time to react if he was correct in his assessment of impending danger. He pulled her away toward a gap in the police barricades by which they stood, but bodies to either side and behind them prevented them from taking more than a few steps.

Just as the cat's descent was about to bring it within reach of Quinn and Ramsey, a tall man pushed his way in front of them. He stretched out both of his arms in an attempt to be a winner and catch the last cat thrown by the Jester.

With a sharp crack the device detonated, and the tall man took the full brunt of the high-explosive blast, becoming an unrecognizable, bleeding lump of flesh. Flying shrapnel from the bomb wounded other bystanders, and yells of pain and panic-stricken screams filled the air. The crowd began a wild stampede in every direction.

As police on the periphery of the crowd drew their guns and raced forward toward the blast site, the Jester on the balcony whipped an AUG submachine gun from the bottom of the bin from which he'd taken his toy cats and opened fire on Quinn and Ramsey. The 5.56 mm hellfire cranked out by the AUG hammered down on the crowd as Quinn and Ramsey zigzagged toward the entrance of the city hall building. Due to distance, windage and angle, though, the AUG fire was inaccurate, cutting down bystanders as they ran away from the scene of the blast.

While Quinn and Ramsey cleared the death zone, the Scorpio termination crew waiting on the fringes pulled blasters from concealed holsters beneath their cat costumes and changed mode from passive surveillance to hot pursuit.

INSIDE the city hall building the Interpol plainclothesmen guarding the man whom they mistakenly believed to be Van Sicklen drew weapons from beneath their coats and hurried toward the balcony where the Jester was firing his automatic weapon down into the crowd.

Having lost track of the male and female investigators he had been intent on killing, the Jester whirled and raised the AUG. Pulling the trigger, he raked the interior of the building with side-to-side, low-trajectory autofire.

The first man to charge the Jester toppled backward, and his service pistol skittered away on the polished terra-cotta floor of the drawing room that led to the balcony.

The officers on either side of the downed man switched from assault to defense as the Jester sprayed the room with more automatic fire. Quickly the costumed killer reloaded another clip of 5.56 mm ammo and fired in the direction of the dodging agents.

As the Interpol men readied for another charge, the Jester threw down his now-dry weapon and pulled two small fragmentation grenades from inside his suit. Arming the conical grenades with a button click on their advanced-design detonators, the Jester held the black epoxy resin cylinders aloft as he bolted headlong into the drawing room toward the lead-throwing Interpol cops.

The two small yet powerful fragmentation submunitions detonated just as the Jester's bullet-riddled body collapsed in a heap near the crouching lawmen. In themselves the grenades weren't powerful enough to cause massive structural damage, but the shaped plastic charges the janitor had planted in the drawing room prior to the festival and following the security sweeps for hidden booby traps were powerful enough to blow the place to kingdom come.

The incendiary explosion ripped through the drawing room, and a seething ball of fire roared toward the balcony, blowing its massive glass doors to jagged splinters amid belching tongues of flame.

Before long the entire top floor of the city hall was ablaze.

QUINN'S LAST GLIMPSE of Ramsey had been of his partner firing a squat black Spectre SMG at the assassins who were crouched on either side of the city hall entrance. Quinn had seen one of the Scorpio hitters blown away by a burst of autofire, then Ramsey had disappeared from view as a police van raced by, its two-note siren blaring.

The sudden fierce explosion from city hall and the twisting coils of noxious black smoke had by then cut Quinn off from any hope of reaching the building, and besides that, he knew full well there was little point in heading that way.

He was convinced Van Sicklen hadn't been the man in the Jester's suit. Nomad was certain the next-to-last surviving scientist had been terminated well before the Jester's appearance on the balcony.

As far as Ramsey went, he would hook up with her sooner or later. He now had another, more immediate concern: staying alive.

From the crowd other Scorpio assassins were springing into violent action. Two masked mercenaries in cat suits were packing lethal heat, directing a lancing stream of rotoring steel Quinn's way.

Bullets whined as they struck the pavement, fragmented and ricocheted off again. Quinn vaulted an iron fence, veered right on a crouch and snapped off a burst of answering SMG fire from the cover of a parade float that sent the shooters scrambling.

From the way one of them limped Quinn saw to his satisfaction that the man had been hit. But two more members of the Scorpio strike force were coming at him fast. Double-teaming him, the first man drew Quinn's fire while the second shooter took careful aim, and Quinn noticed the stubby shape of a rocket grenade fitted to the muzzle of the man's weapon.

The float wouldn't withstand a direct hit by shrapnel hurled from a bursting submunition. Quinn had to take a chance of sustaining a hit on the run or staying put and getting blown all over the landscape.

Throwing a suppressing burst that forced the merc playing decoy to dodge for the cover of a parked car, Quinn prepared to make an all-out dash from ground zero.

Suddenly a compact car raced up, tires screeching as the driver applied the brakes. Quinn saw Ramsey behind the wheel of the Audi. "Get in!" she shouted.

Quinn threw the door open and jumped into the shotgun seat just as a near miss from the rocket round thundered behind them and shook the car.

Ears ringing from the explosion, Quinn jabbed the snub-nosed Spectre SMG out the rolled-down window and opened up on the shooter who was in the process of fitting another rocket onto the barrel of his weapon. Quinn's figure-eight burst cut down the shooter just as he was about to launch the second rocket round.

Ramsey pointed ahead at a car speeding from the scene. "I saw men rush from the building just before the explosion. They got into that Saab and drove away in a big hurry."

The Saab seemed to be crewed by three men. There was the driver in the front seat and two others in back.

The vehicle careened around a corner, losing a hubcap in the process. Ramsey heaved on the steering wheel and gave chase, her eyes widening as she saw an ambulance heading straight for her from the mouth of a narrow intersecting street.

Wrenching the wheel to the other side saved their necks but sent the compact car crashing headlong into the wall of a building. Although the crash only resulted in a badly crumpled right fender, the Saab was nowhere to be seen.

11

"There she goes!"

Quinn had spotted the escaping Saab again just as they were about to admit they had lost the car for keeps. The getaway car was directly ahead of them, taking a turn into a walled town square on a deserted street far from the site of the big parade.

With most of the populace attending the Kattestoet, and the curious and concerned drawn there by reports of what the media were now reporting as a "terrorist strike," it was small wonder that the residential neighborhood that made up this part of the city was deserted.

Few pedestrians were on the streets, and most of the shops were closed for the Belgian festival. Ramsey swung the Audi into the portal leading into the square. Typical of many old Belgian squares, the medieval stone walls that enclosed the plaza were dotted with the windows of apartment units with shop frontage at street level.

On the other side of the wall, facing the plaza, were more shops that could be entered from the square, which on weekends might double as a flea market.

The Saab's wheelman must have spotted the chase car, because midway through the circular plaza the small car picked up speed, its tires squealing on the ancient cobblestone pavement as it swerved to one side and vanished into a narrow side street opening onto the plaza.

Double-clutching while she poured on the gas, Ramsey pushed the Audi to the maximum, finally gaining on the speeding Saab.

Using the Spectres' steel buttstocks to smash the rear window to pieces, the two mercs in the rear of the Saab stuck out their hardware. The SMGs bucked and chattered on full auto, and flame and steel gushed from the gun muzzles as the gunmen opened up on the Audi as it, too, shot into the narrow side street.

While Ramsey smashed down on the accelerator pedal, Quinn stuck his Spectre out the window and triggered a long burst of answering fire, hurling a stream of 9 mm thunderbolts in the Saab's direction. The Saab sprang forward like a frightened colt, outpacing the burst of automatic fire but not evading a hit on one of the rear tires from fragmenting rounds that had ricocheted off the paving cobblestones and adjacent curbstones.

The getaway car careered around a corner onto a main street as the blown tire cost the driver control of the Saab. With one wheel rim grinding against the unevenly paved road surface, the escape vehicle jumped the curb and crashed headlong into the picture window of a flower shop amid a cascade of splintering plate glass.

Dazed but otherwise uninjured, except for superficial cuts, the three Scorpio hit men staggered from the crumpled, steaming wreck. Inside the damaged storefront an old woman emerged from behind the counter to shout curses at the crazy men who had rammed their car into her shop. She grabbed the first merc to come out of the Saab, oblivious to the weapon in his hands.

"Where's your driver's license?" she demanded as she pulled his jacket sleeve. "Look what you've done to my store!"

Shaking off the old woman with ease, the merc smashed the side of the Spectre's steel receiver across the bridge of her nose and sent her crashing into a flower display case, blood streaming down her face.

A split second behind the merc trio Ramsey pulled the Audi to a screaming short stop in front of the flower shop. Quinn took the time to snap a fresh fifty-round high-capacity magazine into the

Spectre as Ramsey pulled a backup Uzi pistol from a shoulder rig worn beneath her windbreaker, preferring the flexibility of the Uzi in a close-quarters tactical situation.

Gunfire greeted the two investigators as they stormed into the shop. They glimpsed the backs of two fleeing figures hustling down a short corridor to one side of the counter that led to the shop's rear entrance. But the third merc spun away from the downed storekeeper to face them head-on.

Caught in the open, the third Scorpio hitter launched a burst at Quinn and Ramsey, which forced them to duck as he made a break for the corridor. But with answering fire singing at his heels from the Uzi and the Spectre, the merc lost his nerve. He changed course before reaching the hall and instead dived for cover behind the counter.

Spooked and abandoned by his partners, the boxed-in shooter completely lost his cool, letting his emotions do the thinking for him instead of his brain. Checking his SMG's clip, he saw that he had twenty more rounds left. He decided to bet the whole pot on making a break for it.

Jumping to his feet, the Scorpio merc threw lead on the fly while he dodged out the open side door of the counter. He figured he could make it to the corridor that gave access to the alleyway behind the flower shop before the two shooters could ventilate him.

The burst forced Quinn and Ramsey to tuck their heads down, but Quinn was on his feet a pulse beat after the erratic fire had ended and went charging off after the running man.

Drawing a fast bead, Quinn cut loose with a 9 mm PB salvo. The result was a near miss only. The hastily aimed multiround burst tore out a chunk of wall to one side of the fleeing gunman as he skidded left and dodged into the corridor, then spun around to snap off another salvo from the Spectre.

Quinn never gave him the chance to pull the trigger.

This time Quinn's accurate fire tattooed a jagged pattern of bloody red tatters across the Scorpio merc's upper chest. Pulverized bone and organ tissue spewed in dark crimson pulses from the exit wounds punched in the merc's back. Reflex action triggered a panic burst that went wild and high, hammering holes in the tin ceiling.

Badly shot up by Spectre fire, the merc crashed into the wall behind him. His knees buckled and he slid slowly down the wall. Hitting bottom with a thunk, he shuddered for a few seconds, then became still.

Quinn and Ramsey pushed past the unmoving body toward the alleyway. Late-afternoon sunlight bright enough to make them wince streamed in through the open back door. They hugged the walls on either side of the doorway, going by the numbers.

Quinn tucked left, back hunched, hitting the outer wall on the fleshy part of his shoulder, waving the Spectre right and left as he straightened to a semicrouch while Ramsey covered him from the side of the doorway with her own armament.

The backyard of the flower shop was deserted. The surviving Scorpio assassins were nowhere to be seen. A ten-foot-high picket fence stretched along the spine of the back alley toward a dead end in a blank brick wall at the right. To the operatives' immediate left, the alley took an eighty-degree dogleg around the corner of the building.

A sizable crowd was already gathering at the shattered frontage of the flower shop. Quinn and Ramsey looked toward the dogleg in the back alley as voices from the street shouted behind them angrily in Flemish and Walloon.

Around the corner of the alley the other two Scorpio mercs were waiting in ambush, mat-black steel bulging in their fists, ready to dole out punishing autofire. Wound tight, the spooked shooters opened up right away, not even bothering to wait for Ramsey and Quinn to completely clear the back alley and walk directly into the killbox.

That was their mistake, and one they would wind up paying the Reaper for. The mercs' premature assault fire gave their targets enough reaction time to duck back around the projecting rim of the building, narrowly evading a scything brace of PB rivets.

Hugging the wall, Quinn stuck the snout of his SMG around the corner and rotored out a long, blind burst. Sent scrambling by the sudden fire, the mercs were just popping back up to launch another salvo when Quinn and Ramsey jumped out into view with their weapons at their hips, spraying the alley with whipsawing steel.

Outmaneuvered, the trapped merc hit men didn't even have enough time to yank their triggers. The deadly swarm of whizzing steel shredders walloped into their bodies. Nailed where they stood, the dying men staggered for a moment, then collapsed in blood-spattered jumbles.

Quinn and Ramsey had made them ante up.

Big time.

IT WAS COLD in the morgue, cold as any meat freezer, Quinn thought as he and Ramsey entered in the company of the mortician. Metal shelves stacked up against the glazed cinder-block walls were crammed with toe-tagged bodies in transparent zippered bags.

The high body count didn't go with the picture-postcard architecture, the spotless mass transit and the quaint cafés on picturesque squares, but Brussels was a city of many sides.

It was a city of paradoxes, renowned as much as a market for gemstones as an international clearinghouse for sophisticated small arms and classified military documents. Its sleepy exterior belied a metropolis where dark undercurrents had flowed for centuries and still did today.

The mortician directed Quinn and Ramsey to one of the freezer compartments and trundled out the stainless-steel slab. The charred remains of Gropius Van Sicklen lay on the slab. The blackened lump of carbon was unrecognizable as anything that had once been human, let alone one of the most prestigious scientists in the world, but the dental work and an implant from earlier hip surgery had positively identified the body as Van Sicklen.

The scientist's housekeeper had taken off by the time Quinn and his partner arrived back at Van Sicklen's residence. Quinn immediately checked Van Sicklen's computer workstation data bank for any clue to why he'd been murdered.

As Quinn had suspected, the data bank had been bulk-erased—every byte had been zeroed out, permitting no possibility of recovery. The woman known as "Mrs. Haagen" had put her escape plan into operation immediately. Undoubtedly she was now miles away from the strike zone.

There was little chance she'd be found, since despite Van Sicklen's obvious long-standing relationship with his cherished housekeeper, there wasn't a single scrap of data on her anywhere in the world's intelligence computers.

Quinn removed a data module from his pocket and inserted it into one of the computer's free slots. It contained a powerful unerase utility of his own devising that could sometimes recapture data even from erased mass storage devices. The unerase program loaded, Quinn waited for it to cycle through its routines.

From the depths of the computer's wiped memory the unerase utility dredged up only a single scrap of data a few bytes in size. The data string was a recognizable word.

The word was CASTLE.

QUINN PLACED the raster in sleep mode. He had spent most of the previous day conducting a full-spectrum search of the world's computer data bases. Billions of bytes of data had been sifted through electronic filters programmed to collate any and all references to Castle.

He had obtained clearances for and sifted through not only the top-secret data bases of Interpol, the National Security Agency, the CIA, Israeli Mossad, Egyptian Mukhabarat, French DGI, German BND, but a host of semiprivate university think tanks, too, and had turned up thousands of references to Castle. Not a single one of these, however, could even remotely have any significance to the Prometheus kills.

Sophisticated AI, artificial-intelligence-based screening software, had sifted through every reference at lightning speed, but nowhere in the vast compendium of text and visuals could the program offer Quinn the match of ninety percent or greater that he had requested of it.

Quinn had reached yet another dead end.

Was Castle an actual reference to an important lead? he wondered. Or was it merely a random glitch in the bulk-erase procedure used to wipe Van Sicklen's data bank? Could it have even been planted there by the mysterious yet deadly opposition as a red herring to throw him off or as bait to lead him into a trap?

Quinn had no idea. Nothing made sense anymore. All Quinn knew was that men were dying all across the globe. There was a link to those hits and to the numerous attempts on the lives of himself and Ramsey. That link existed. That much he knew.

Whether or not Castle was part of the equation, Quinn couldn't say yet. But right now he needed something else. His brain felt squeezed and his eyes were aching. He needed sleep.

12

Wilhelm Koenig walked the grounds of his sprawling country estate with his prize falcon on his arm. The hunting lodge had originally been built by Hermann Göring, who had founded the infamous Nazi Gestapo during the heyday of Hitler's Germany.

Like everything the inventor of the Prometheus Net did, acquiring Göring's hunting lodge for his personal estate was a controversial move, one he knew beforehand was guaranteed to stoke the rumor mills of the world media.

The media had been abuzz that he was acquiring the estate of one of Nazi Germany's greatest war criminals, a man who had taken cyanide at the Nuremberg trials rather than face the hangman's harsh though well-deserved retribution.

Koenig had brushed off all charges of insensitivity that had been leveled against him. He, like Germany itself, wasn't concerned with the excesses and crimes of the Nazi past, only with the potential for a better future.

He was an avid hunter, and the vast estate was perfectly suited to his needs. The hunting lodge was situated in prime Bavarian hill country. Its seclusion afforded him the peace and tranquillity that he required to conduct his work.

Now this hard-won tranquillity had been broken by a chain of unforeseen disasters that had violently claimed the lives of the international scientific committee that had brought his dream within an ace of being realized.

One couldn't see the small army of intelligence operatives and Bundeswehr policemen, nor could one discern the vast array of detection devices that they had placed everywhere around the perimeter of the estate to guard against intrusion by terrorists, but Koenig's hidden guardians were there just the same.

Koenig was a virtual prisoner on his own estate. The irony of this happening to the very man who many claimed would liberate mankind from its dependence on fossil fuels and potentially destructive nuclear energy wasn't lost on him.

Reluctantly Koenig had recognized the necessity for the presence of his protectors. He was no stranger to compromise, and once Prometheus was on-line he wouldn't care a bit about his personal fate in any event.

He had realized that much of the cause of war in modern times hadn't been land, as dictators and demagogues had long claimed. Instead, Koenig had formulated the theory that mankind's hunger for sources of energy was the true reason for war and its attendant evils.

In the closing years of the twentieth century the world's superpowers had been poised to conduct a bloody clash over the precious oil reserves beneath the sands of the Middle East. The crisis had been resolved only when a miscalculating Saddam Hussein had made the monumental blunder of invading nearby Kuwait at the precise point in history when the arsenal of the West was at its peak strength. Having sown the wind, the Iraqi dictator had reaped the whirlwind when the Western democracies chose to fight instead of backing down.

All the same, mankind's need for energy sources had brought it perilously close to Armageddon. Had Saddam Hussein possessed a nuclear capability the pages of history might have recorded a far bloodier confrontation than what had actually taken place.

Even before Kuwait there had been nuclear power plant accidents such as the ones at Chernobyl and Three Mile Island, both of which demonstrated that even in peacetime nuclear reactors could unleash disaster on a widespread scale. So Koenig had reasoned that freeing mankind from energy dependence might mean freeing it from war, as well. Armed with this conviction, he devoted his adult years to championing the Prometheus Net concept.

And now, in the end, his beloved Prometheus Project itself might kill him. Very well, then, Koenig thought. Let it. Koenig released the falcon and watched it soar into the air. He thought about Yeats's great poem "The Second Coming."

In it the poet spoke about a new golden age beckoning mankind, but he also warned against the potential for destruction on a grand scale. What rough beast was now slouching toward Bethlehem? Koenig wondered. What new threat could be foretold in the falcon's widening gyre?

THE ONE CALLED ALPHA faced the glowing screen of the computer terminal. The screen showed him a face. It was the face that was telling Alpha things that he didn't want to hear.

Taurus was falling down on the job. That was the bottom line. Sagittarius and Scorpio had already paid the ultimate price for their unpardonable failures.

But Taurus was a different matter entirely. Taurus was Alpha's right-hand merc. As such, he was judged by a different standard than the others.

Alpha had personally selected Taurus to oversee the entire Daybreak operation. Ultimately any setbacks that the op suffered were Taurus's direct responsibility.

Alpha didn't like hearing things that didn't please him, especially when they concerned Daybreak. The merc on the other end of the screen knew that all too well.

"It's not my fault," the merc code-named Taurus informed Alpha. "The ground assets talked a better fight than they put out."

"We are growing impatient," Alpha's electronic voice said to the face on the screen. "You must not again incur our displeasure."

The eyes in the face on the screen blinked frantically. The mouth churned as the brain of Taurus cast about for the right words, words that wouldn't antagonize Alpha any more than he already was.

"Don't worry. It won't happen again. I promise you it won't," the merc stressed.

There was bravado in the voice, but in the end it was hollow, a lying voice without the power to convince. Voice stress analysis corroborated Alpha's gut feeling. Retinal analysis readings confirmed the observational results.

What a loathsome, treacherous maggot Taurus was, Alpha thought. Wasn't the merc aware that Alpha knew what he thought before Taurus himself even thought it?

Taurus had been useful to Alpha in the early phases of his initiative. The merc had been instrumental in collecting intelligence needed to blackmail the right people into supplying the money, political pressure and technology necessary to build his criminal power base.

He had also supplied Alpha with Genesis, the sport killer who had been highly effective in conducting strategic hits against those who knew too much or who wouldn't cooperate with Alpha's plans for a new world order.

Now, though, Alpha was beginning to doubt that Taurus had what it took to be part of the program. Daybreak was far too important, far too big, to allow substandard personnel to play a hand. Alpha would allow his merc catspaw one more chance to carry out the termination directive without screwing up.

And then he would deal with him.

As he had dealt with the others.

As he would eventually deal with anyone or anything that opposed his will.

THE MESSAGE FLASHED onto the screen. WARN-ING! CHECKSUM ERROR.

The CERT tech in the CPU node threw up his arms in exasperation as he pushed his chair away from the data screen at which he sat. The damn checksum always kept coming up wrong.

Whatever kind of bug had taken control of the command-and-control computer's file allocation tables, boot sector and other critical elements of the software operating system, it seemed impervious to every countermeasure they had tried.

Each checksum routine—a program that counted the number of data bytes in the system, reflecting changes in the data logged on the software and verifying its integrity—came up showing different results.

Checksum errors were to computer viruses what high temperatures were in human beings. Each indicated that a bug was still running rampant in the system.

Suddenly a warning alarm sounded. The tech looked up and realized what was happening. The glowing characters flashing on one of the big view screens on the wall said it all.

STRIKE SYSTEM ACTIVATED.

The doomsday scenario had finally been triggered, he now knew. The viral invader in the computer system had triggered STRIKE. The automated antiterrorist system would bring lasers and other advanced-design weapons systems immediately into play.

STRIKE's artificial-intelligence-driven, fail-soft, fault-tolerant weapon interface would be ready to hunt down and eradicate anything it identified as hostile.

The Prometheus computer's central processing unit, its CPU, was STRIKE's high-priority defense zone. It was at the CPU that the CERT tech was working.

The tech was immediately on his feet, running toward the elevator bank a few hundred feet away at the end of the corridor, but before he reached it he saw that the doors were already closing as STRIKE sealed the CPU off from what it mistakenly believed was a terrorist attack.

From the muzzle of a laser pulse gun high on the wall of the CPU chamber a coherent beam of lethal red light lanced out with computer-targeted accuracy as the CERT man reached the elevator. The twenty-megawatt laser burst arrowed through his heart with the precision of a surgeon's scalpel, cauterizing flesh and making blood boil in his ventricles and auricles. Identifying the technician as a terrorist saboteur, STRIKE had carried out its mandate to acquire and then immediately destroy the target.

The rest of the CERT unit fled from the heart of the central processing unit to one of the remote-access stations where slave data terminals were located. From there they could still feed data to the CPU. The core of the computer system, though, was off-limits now.

STRIKE was armed. It was ready to eradicate anything that moved, just as the body's defense system was primed to destroy any microbic invader. The data virus had now bored deeper into the silicon microchips that made up the inner regions of the computer's brain.

And driven it mad.

13

"Mr. Quinn!" the bald man in the dark business suit called out while he waved his hand over his head. "This way, please. I'm called Choy," the stranger added as Quinn and Ramsey approached him. "Dr. Zhou sent me to meet you."

They all shook hands, then Choy picked up Ramsey's flight bag and gestured toward the interior of the departure terminal.

"Come with me, please," he said. "I have a limousine waiting outside to take you to your destination."

"And precisely where would that be?" Quinn asked. "Dr. Zhou left no instructions that we were to be met by anyone at the airport. As far as I know, we were to phone to confirm a meeting this evening."

"I regret that won't be possible. The doctor has been called away on urgent business on the mainland. He won't be available to consult with you until tomorrow morning. However, everything has been arranged to provide for your comfort until then. Please come."

Quinn had learned long ago to trust his instincts, and these told him that Choy was on the level. The eyes of corrupt men held deception. Choy's didn't.

"Okay," Quinn said, shouldering his own bag. "Let's go."

The car that Choy had waiting for the investigators sent by the Interpol-affiliated task force was a Mercedes town car. Cracking the door for Ramsey, Choy placed their baggage in the trunk of the Mercedes, then climbed behind the wheel. The heat of the tropical day was soon dispelled by the cool crispness of the vehicle's air-conditioned interior.

Choy drove from the terminal and out onto the main highway where he accelerated to a cruising speed of seventy miles per hour. The route signs they passed indicated that they were heading toward the center of Hong Kong, whose skyscrapers were visible against a backdrop of spectacular mountains.

Although the Chinese Communists had taken over the former British protectorate in 1997, even the conservative Reds hadn't been stubborn enough to obstruct Hong Kong's potential as a capitalist city-state. Faced with the threat of a massive flight of capital and technology to other parts of the Pacific Rim that had been gathering steam for years prior to the changeover, the Communists had left much of Hong Kong's economic infrastructure unchanged.

"Dr. Zhou has left instructions that you're to be made guests in his house," Choy said as he idled down after shifting into the left lane. "You'll have the run of the place in his absence with all amenities available to you."

"How far is it to the doctor's place?" Ramsey asked.

"It isn't far," Choy replied as he slid into the right lane after passing a turnoff sign. "We'll be there in only a few more minutes."

Dr. Zhou's house turned out to be one of the mansions perched on the heights above Repulse Bay. Choy rolled up a narrow dirt access road and parked the car in the mansion's garage. He exited the limo, got their baggage out and ushered them into the house.

The interior of the house was as well appointed as its exterior was elegant. Zhou's mansion was decorated with taste and style in the classical European tradition of a bygone age. One wall of the living room, dominated by an immense, flat high-definition TV screen, served as the media center, and Choy gave them a quick rundown on how to use the console.

"Dr. Zhou has programmed a brief message for you," Choy said, indicating the media center's console. "Please play it at your earliest convenience. As for the rest," he added, "don't hesitate to phone me if there's anything else I can do for you. I can be reached directly at the press of a call button."

"When can we meet the doctor?" Quinn asked as he was handed the keys to the house and the Mercedes.

"All of that information is contained in the doctor's message," Choy politely told him before turning to leave. "It will adequately answer all your questions."

Moments later Quinn watched Choy pull a small Japanese compact from the car park and drive down onto the highway.

In a short while, Dr. Zhou's face filled the large screen. Quinn and Ramsey watched and listened to his message.

The doctor explained that he had been called away from his work on important business in Beijing. One didn't question the wisdom of the political elite on the mainland, and so the doctor had left with little advance notice. Zhou apologized for the inconvenience to the United Nations' emissaries, but it couldn't be helped.

He could assure them, however, that he would be available to answer any questions they had regarding Prometheus promptly the following morning.

He would be waiting for them at his residence on Shantung Island, one of the outer islands of the former Hong Kong colony that had been renamed since the '97 takeover. Choy would come to fetch them first thing in the morning, whereupon they would be shuttled to the island on the *Lao Tzu,* Zhou's private hydrofoil docked at the marina.

"I'm starved," Quinn told Ramsey after they listened to Zhou's prerecorded message. "How about we head into Kowloon and grab some dinner? Unless things have changed drastically since the Chinese takeover, there's a place that serves the best snake on the island."

"I know the place you mean," Ramsey countered. "It's the Snake King Moon in Snake Alley. I've dined there often myself."

Quinn slid behind the wheel of the Mercedes and tooled the superbly crafted German car onto the highway. Zhou's house was located minutes away from where the action was in Hong Kong, and the road signs were still mostly in English. They found a place to park on Nathan Road and walked the short distance to Snake Alley, a small street renowned for its many snake restaurants.

Neon blazed on the main drag, but the narrow street that Quinn and Ramsey turned onto was poorly lit. As they entered, Quinn got the feeling that unseen watchers were lurking in the shadows.

But when he turned, he could see no one following them. He attributed his unease to the unanticipated violence that had interfered with the investigation since its start in Rome. When the opposition played hardball, as on this case, expecting trouble could indicate a healthy state of mind.

Quinn found the Snake King Moon exactly where he'd remembered it. The small restaurant's nondescript exterior would have been overlooked by any passerby not knowing precisely where to look. It bore no sign, and there was no other indiction that the shop front with black-painted windows was even an active business.

Quinn pushed open the door and was immediately surrounded by the hustle and bustle of a busy restaurant at the dinner hour. The smiling Chinese waiter ushered them in and seated them at the darkened rear at one of the few tables that weren't occupied by patrons.

After placing their orders, Quinn and Ramsey drank native beer while they waited for the food to be served. They dined on snake breast meat stuffed with shelled shrimp and stir-fried shredded snake served with braised chicken liver, then called for the check. The waiter soon brought them a domed serving dish on a silver tray.

"Dessert is compliments of the house," he said as he set the tray down on a serving table and lifted the lid. Beneath it lay a Walther autopistol. Before Quinn or Ramsey could react the waiter had the gun in his hand. He had the drop on the pair of agents and was about to squeeze the trigger when a man stepped quickly behind him and jammed a finely honed ice pick into his ear with expert skill.

The waiter grunted and collapsed as the man grabbed the Walther and steered the sagging Chinese toward a vacant booth, then turned to face Quinn and Ramsey. His florid face broke into a grin.

"That's one you owe me, partner," Bruckner told Quinn as he scanned the restaurant. Few had noticed the commotion at the darkened rear of the room, and patrons and management were only now beginning to glance their way with a mixture of curiosity and fear. "Now let's get out of here. We've got to talk."

With Bruckner in tow they hustled to their car and were soon lost in the maze of narrow streets feeding off Nathan Road. A few minutes later they pulled into another narrow alley, where Bruckner indicated a door they were to enter.

The door led to a corridor reeking of a mixture of various odors, none of them pleasant. A room opened off the corridor. It was crammed with sophisticated command, control, communications and intelligence gear.

"The place is ELINT-shielded and blast-hardened," Bruckner said as he seated himself on one of the chairs placed here and there. He gestured to the two operatives, indicating they should seat themselves, too. "We can talk here."

"Talk about what?" asked Quinn, who remained standing.

"There's a lot to brief you on," Bruckner responded. "The first thing concerns the Prometheus command-and-control computer. What the CERT technicians first thought was the data bug was discovered a few days ago. Turns out that it's more like a 'worm' than the simple Trojan they first believed."

Bruckner went on to explain how the CERT team made up of the world's top computer specialists was at work at that moment trying to purge the ground control system of the rogue viral program.

The big problem was that the computer had armed STRIKE. With the computer's perimeter defensive system on the alert, the underground complex in Storm King Mountain had been turned into a fully mechanized deathtrap.

If anyone was aware of the potential of STRIKE, it was Quinn, who had designed STRIKE from the ground up. Bruckner wanted to know now if there was any way to neutralize the system.

"Sure there is," Quinn told him. "Just turn it off. The computer has a security clearance code engineered into the architecture for just such a contingency. It's a built-in fail-safe feature."

Bruckner shook his head. "No can do, kemo sabe," he answered with a shake of his head. "The virus—or whatever the fuck it is—has overridden the fail-safe feature. It's closed every electronic back door into the system right in the programmers' faces. The entire system is locked down and completely self-contained."

"Then at this point my advice to you is to continue trying to purge the system of the virus. Don't challenge STRIKE except as a last resort. It's lethal. I know. I made STRIKE."

"That's what I was afraid you would say," Bruckner returned. Then, with a shrug, he added, "Okay. I'll inform the CERT techs of what you just told me. Now it's your turn. Bring me up to date."

Quinn and Ramsey briefed Bruckner on the events in Rome, Brussels and most recently in Hong Kong. They explained that Zhou would meet with them the following morning.

Bruckner sent the record of the conversation to the special command post beneath the White House via secure-coded facsimile from where it would be unscrambled and disseminated to the UN-mandated Prometheus task force.

"One final point," Bruckner said before Quinn and Ramsey left the covert command center. "Koenig is now under twenty-four-hour guard at a remote mountain estate. The Germans don't want anything happening to their hero of the moment. Koenig didn't like it, but the Germans wouldn't hear of it. It's the heaviest security effort since they threw Albert Speer into Spandau Prison.''

Quinn hoped it would be good enough to save Koenig's life.

14

The next morning Choy appeared at Zhou's mansion, ready to drive his employer's guests to the marina. Quinn and Ramsey were already waiting for him.

Dr. Zhou's Man Friday drove the town car with the windows rolled down, since the morning was still cool. It was late morning by the time they reached the marina forty minutes later. The subtropical air was already beginning to turn hot and humid.

"There," Choy remarked, pointing to a sleek, low-draft craft berthed at one of the slips. "The captain should already be on board and the *Lao Tzu* ready for immediate departure."

"The *Lao Tzu*," Quinn mused aloud. "Named after the ancient Chinese philosopher."

"Quite so," Choy answered. "Dr. Zhou is a believer in the ancient Way. He claims that it is the only religion compatible with the modern scientific age, an age in which man is reduced to a mere spectator of cosmic events."

"Zhou sounds like an interesting man," Ramsey put in.

"He is," Choy replied as he stepped back from the boarding plank. "Please come aboard."

The high-pitched keening of the hydrofoil's powerful turbines filled the air as the engines idled prior to departure.

Choy took the agents forward into the wheelhouse and introduced them to the captain, an amiable Chinese named Lu. The captain declared that the craft was ready to leave the slip.

Choy and Quinn hauled in the lines, and the *Lao Tzu* slowly began to pull away from the marina.

"Until we clear the channel and reach open water we'll use the turbines for propulsion in hullborne mode," Choy explained. He pointed ahead to indicate the deep-water channel demarcated by a procession of large buoys that stretched out in a gentle S-curve into the middle of the water beyond the mainland of Hong Kong.

In the distance the blue-gray shapes of the outer islands were visible against the horizon, appearing much farther away than they actually were. "Once we clear the channel," Choy continued, "we can extend the hydrofoils and achieve maximum speed."

"Travel time?" Ramsey asked.

"Approximately twenty-five minutes," the captain responded, "depending on the wind and the tides."

"How secure is a craft like this?" Quinn asked, noting that there was a great deal of open water lying between the Hong Kong mainland and their destination, Shantung Island. "In twenty-five minutes a hell of a lot can happen."

"Quite so," Choy returned with a smile. "We're well aware of this fact. That's why several security measures have been engineered into this custom-built craft. The hull, for example, is constructed of a special thermoplastic polymer, hard yet lightweight. All windows are capable of withstanding high-explosive strikes and are impervious to shrapnel. As for speed, you'll witness for yourself the abilities of this craft once the channel is cleared."

"Impressive," Quinn admitted.

"Ah, but there's more," Choy went on, his smile growing broader still. "Come below. I'll be pleased to show you."

Choy took Quinn aft and then down into a compartment below the deck. The compartment took the form of a narrow cylinder, a vertical steel tube.

be there stood a black leather swivel
was fastened to the deck by a circle of
d its base. A visored helmet and gloves
abric lay on the cushion of the chair.

"Here's what makes the *Lao Tzu* impregnable," Choy said with pride. "Its fire control system. The helmet features an eye-motion responsive virtual-reality strike management interface with the on-board computer controlling the craft's defensive system. Armament includes Exocet missiles, a 20 mm Vulcan cannon and HARM antiradar warheads. All of these can be actuated by means of the VRSM interface. I'll demonstrate."

Strapping himself into the chair, Choy keystroked his protected access code into a small keypad on the armrest and put on the helmet and gloves. At the same time, the chair rose on a pneumatic lift, and cantilevered blast shields made of high-carbon steel retracted with a whirr overhead to reveal a transparent hyperpolymer dome that was both bulletproof and blastproof.

"Now I'm really impressed," Quinn admitted to Choy, grasping the principle behind the *Lao Tzu*'s battle management system.

Strapped into the catbird seat, the weapon controller commanded a full 360-degree view onto which could be superimposed a computer-generated, real-time, virtual-reality threat display as well as available counterthreat options.

Both eye motions and gloves would enable the wearer to punch virtual "buttons" that would lock on and fire individual weapons systems selected from computer-generated icons. The flexing of hand muscles inside the touch-sensitive gloves would produce an electronic feedback signal that would cause either hand's virtual counterpart to activate any or all of the weapons icons on the display and launch them into action.

"As you can see," Choy told Quinn after he lowered the command chair, powered down the system and stepped back onto the deck, "the craft is formidably armed and well secured. We're quite safe on board the *Lao Tzu*."

THE MICROSUB CARRYING strike team Aquarius One stole through the murky waters of the broad deep-water channel. Augmented by noise reduction technology, its powerful turbine engine gave the undersea personnel delivery craft the speed and lethal silence of a predatory shark. The microsub had been following the *Lao Tzu* since the moment she had slid from her berth and angled her prow into the channel.

Three scuba-suited mercs with the stubby profiles of closed-circuit breathing apparatus on their
backs were on board the covert assault sub.
Scrubbed of the least trace of carbon dioxide, ni-
trogen and other blood contaminants, the recy-
cled air would generate no telltale bubbles that
might give away the presence of the divers below.

The gear ported by the two divers also included
silenced automatic weapons highly resistant to the
harmful effects of exposure to seawater. The
weapons wouldn't be required until the men had
resurfaced and would remain safe until then.

The black torpedo-shaped undersea personnel
delivery craft pulled broadside of the keel of the
Lao Tzu's hard-chine displacement hull as the
vessel knifed a churning white swath through the
channel's waters.

The merc detail had planned the timetable for
the strike to perfection, cognizant of the fact that
only minutes remained before the hydrofoil
cleared the channel and was out in the open sea.
Once this transition occurred and the craft shunted
from conventional turbine power to hydrofoil
propulsion, the *Lao Tzu*'s hull would be lifted
above the waterline and be moving at far too great
a speed for them to overtake in the microsub.

Embarkation of the target craft would have to be accomplished before that time.

As far as Aquarius One went, this wouldn't be a problem. The underwater duo was already swimming free of the microsub, adhering to the *Lao Tzu*'s keel by pneumatic grapnel devices resembling large black suction cups that were strapped to wrists and knees.

Moments later the two Aquarius strikers were clambering up over the gunwale of the *Lao Tzu*. The sound of their arrival masked by the throbbing of the craft's powerful engines and the noise of the salt wake, they boarded the *Lao Tzu* amidships and immediately unshipped their weapons.

Soon silenced automatic hardware bulked in their gloved fists. Their tanks, masks and fins now stowed near the points where they had boarded, the two wet-suited mercs communicated by hand signals which targets in the wheelhouse dead ahead each striker was to take out.

Weapons in hand, they began moving stealthily toward the wheelhouse.

15

The merc shooter mouthed a silent curse. The yawing of the vessel's deck was adversely affecting his aim. He gripped the bullpup-configured close-assault weapon firmly in both hands and sighted on his target through the reticule at the center of the top-mounted scope.

He assumed a more stable stance and tried to sight again. This time he got his man in line for a head shot, took a deep breath and began squeezing off a round.

A sudden swell picked up the vessel and tossed it to one side as the bolt slammed into the firing pin and the round was discharged from the muzzle of the CAW. Even as the merc triggered a second round he knew he had blown his chance.

Burrowing into the deck instead of striking its target, the round alerted Quinn instead of killing him. Reflexes shunted Quinn into combat mode. Thought gave way to action.

Nomad was already diving for cover as he heard the crack of the first round, and then heard the thud of the second round wallop into the instrument panel behind him.

From a crouch Quinn glimpsed the two figures in black wet suits who had climbed aboard the *Lao Tzu*. The element of surprise they had counted on wasn't a valuable asset anymore. Switching their hardware from select fire to fully automatic, the Aquarius terminators were now going for the overkill option.

Resighting the bullpup-configured assault weapon, the Aquarius terminator prepared to open up again with a three-round salvo of caseless steel that would cycle out at 450 rounds per minute.

As he swung the truncated black plastic weapon to hip level, the *Lao Tzu*'s captain cleared the channel and was out in open ocean. The craft's computer-controlled automatic pilot instantly shunted over from standard-prop turbopower into hydrofoil-propulsion mode.

The *Lao Tzu* surged forward as its speed increased fivefold. Lift buoyancy raised its prow and keel off the level of surface chop on forward and aft hydrofoils. The sudden shift into high-speed mode pitched the two Aquarius strikers roughly to one side, toppling them over and spoiling any chances of drawing an accurate bead on their targets.

Drenched with icy sea spray, the first of the merc hitters to regain his balance rose to a one-knee crouch and managed to bring his weapon into play. A burst of 4.73 mm caseless ammo flew wide of its mark, splintering the thermoplastic hull of the speeding craft but doing little other damage as it missed its intended victim by several feet.

"Hold her steady!" Quinn yelled at the captain as he whipped advanced-design hardware of his own from beneath his windbreaker. Loaded with 5.70 mm high-velocity rounds, the doughnut-shaped P90 close-assault weapon was ready for full-auto deployment.

The *Lao Tzu*'s captain signaled to Quinn, holding up two splayed fingers to indicate assent. He was doing his level best to pour on the steam, pulling the throttles wide open and keeping the craft on course.

Quinn dropped one of the two strikers with a burst from the P90 CAW. The three-round butterfly of spinning steel punched its way through heart and lung tissue at high velocity with punishing force.

As the slugs impacted on their targets, Merc One was hurled to one side. Hydrostatic shock of rapid energy transfer from flying metal to stationary human tissue caused his lungs and spleen to break apart inside his body with rupturing force. A gaping exit wound was testament to the killing power of the 5.70s. He toppled over sideways, teetered for a moment on the verge of plunging into the foaming wake of the speeding craft, then was swept to his death in a cloud of spray.

The second merc was still in action, though, and making definite moves to survive the unforeseen crimp in Aquarius One's neatly plotted tactical scenario. The small black APERS grenade he pulled from a clip on the utility belt at his waist was a deadly antipersonnel submunition with a wide splinter radius.

The merc pitched the grenade, and Nomad dived to one side, taking cover behind a bulkhead before the grenade exploded and a deadly cocoon of preformed steel shrapnel showered the impact zone.

Quinn was up and throwing lethal heat a moment later. Part of the zigzagging P90 burst caught the second merc across the belly, almost chopping him in half. The man in the wet suit did a spastic dance as his life spewed out in a red gush, then he slid down to the deck and landed on his face.

Quinn heaved the limp form of the terminated hitter over the side of the Lao Tzu and immediately rushed back to the prow of the speeding craft. He found the helmsman collapsed against the pilot's seat and Choy lying on the deck nearby, with Ramsey crouching next to him.

While unsuccessful in achieving its primary objectives, the assault of Aquarius One had claimed some victims nonetheless. Slug fragments from the bullpup assault weapons had severed one of the major arteries in Choy's neck, and he was now permanently out of the running.

"Choy gave me the access code for the boat's defense system before he caught a slug," Ramsey said. She hastily relayed the alphanumeric code to Quinn.

Quinn had a hunch that the *Lao Tzu*'s defense system would prove to be necessary before too long. The assassination try had obviously been designed to go down quickly and with a minimum of force expended.

Quinn knew that if he himself had planned the takeout party, he would certainly have backup waiting in the wings in case the operation turned sour. Soon that backup was due to arrive on the scene.

"I see something!" Ramsey shouted, pointing to starboard as the hydrofoil roared past two small islands—more like big, partially submerged rocks—that lay just beyond the mouth of the channel.

Three sleek black CAT-type low-draft pursuit raft had suddenly appeared. They had apparbeen berthed behind the concealment of the lands, ready to take over after the *Lao Tzu* channel in the event that the two-man carry out their mission.

Ra at the second wave of fast-closing termina What do we do now? Turn back?"

"Negative," Quinn replied with a shake of his head, casting an anxious glance at the pursuit craft, which were drawing closer with each passing second. He knew that turning back now would be playing right into the hands of the enemy. "Can you keep her on course?"

"Yes, I think so. According to what the captain told me, the *Lao Tzu* has a sophisticated computer navigation system. She'll take us automatically to our destination. I just have to keep an eye on the controls."

"Do that," Quinn said to Ramsey. "I'm going below deck to see what kind of armament this thing has."

Quinn was down below a couple of seconds later. Using the access code and following the procedures that Choy had used in his demonstration of the ship's on-board VRSM system, Quinn strapped himself into the catbird seat and pla the virtual-reality helmet on his head afte ning the gloves. The chair moved upwar cantilevered armored blast shield slid the shrapnel-proof observation do

Now, through the clear hy Quinn could see the chase *Lao Tzu*. Studding the fir tem to life, Quinn immediately saw a multicolored graphical computer display superimposed above the real-world scene visible to his naked eyes, almost like a translucent film overlay.

As the defense system's laser target designators electronically interrogated all hardware in the area using IFF conventions and locked on to the threats, each of the three speedboats on Quinn's tail appeared on his virtual-reality screen designated as colored icons.

Both the threat icons and the icon representing the *Lao Tzu* were accurately shown with respect to their actual speeds and positions. To the left and right axes of the virtual eyes-up display, columns of numerical readouts flashed constantly updated information pertaining to speed, estimated time of contact and other pertinent tactical data.

At the bottom end of the computer-generated tactical display a row of icons represented the various weapons available to Quinn, including 20 mm Vulcan fire, HARM antiradar missiles and Exocet sea-skimming antiship rockets. A flashing arrow cursor could be moved to any of the weapons icons at will as the cursor responded to the movement of Quinn's eyeballs. When the weapons icon was highlighted by the cursor, the weapon could be activated and fired at any of the targets, identifying the weapons deployed against it.

Three hundred yards behind the *Lao Tzu*, the operations manager on board the point craft shouted into the compact common unit clutched in his hand. The merc code-named Aquarius ordered the two other craft to hold their fire. His point craft would be the one to initiate contact.

Aquarius next commanded the other mercs to deploy one of the man-portable SMAWs, shoulder-launched, multipurpose assault weapon systems carried on board. The SMAW fired a variety of warheads for an assortment of combat roles.

The SMAW tube now ported by the merc in the speedboat was equipped with a laser-guided, heat-seeking warhead.

Once the shooter acquired the target, seeing the prompt in his scope reticle, he depressed the trigger. The warhead whooshed from the SMAW's muzzle in a flash as its stabilizer vanes snapped into position. The on-board IR sensor took over, terminally guiding the missile to the engine of the *Lao Tzu* with yawing burns of rocket exhaust.

Quinn saw the yellow flash on the icon of the lead pursuit craft, which quickly turned into an icon of a missile in flight. A broken line of glowing dashes signaled the computer's projection of the SMAW round's attack-profile envelope.

By means of eye motions Quinn immediately moved his weapons control cursor across the screen, merged it with the icon representing the Vulcan cannon and selected the Vulcan by clicking on the icon. The message beside the icon flashed READY.

The high-tech version of the Gatling gun was capable of setting up a flak front of 20 mm armor-piercing hard-core rounds. The APHCs were capable of detonating any incoming warhead before it reached its target.

With a solid computer lock on the incoming SMAW round, the Vulcan gun began spitting out 20 mm APHCs, targeting in on the SMAW warhead with constant updates on speed and trajectory of the ICW.

The SMAW warhead vectored directly into the cloud of spinning APHCs thrown up by the Vulcan cannon. As a result of the intervention of Vulcan fire, the SMAW's IR seeker head sustained a direct frontal burst, resulting in an explosion that disintegrated the SMAW round in a flash of incandescence. The CAT high-speed interceptor craft skimmed the surface of the sea through the low-hanging pall of noxious black smoke and intense heat generated by the explosion.

The operations manager on board the lead craft, code-named Aquarius, had been briefed that the *Lao Tzu* was equipped with sophisticated defensive equipment. He had intended the first strike as a trial balloon, a live-fire test of the system's counterthreat capability.

Through compact field glasses the Aquarius commander saw that more firepower was needed to blow the *Lao Tzu* out of the water. He quickly ordered two more SMAWs to be loaded with IR-seeking, terminally guided munitions and fired at the swiftly moving escape craft ahead of his waterborne strike unit. In addition the electrically powered GE miniguns mounted on the sleek prows of all three CATs were to commence throwing their high-velocity 7.62 mm automatic fire at the *Lao Tzu*.

As the SMAW birds left their pipes, Quinn found himself confronted with a multitude of threat variables on his virtual screen. Several weapons at once were being fired at him, and the electronic environment was cluttered.

Sweat gathered on Quinn's brow as he struggled to counter the multiple threats. Although he deployed Vulcan and a variety of missiles, one SMAW exploded close enough to the *Lao Tzu* to damage its aft hydrofoil. The speeding vessel shuddered as it violently slewed to one side before navigational computers corrected trim.

"Quinn!" he heard Ramsey's urgent voice in his headset. "Can you hear me?"

"Loud and clear!"

"We're losing power," she shouted. "I think that last strike sheared off part of our aft foil."

"Keep her moving. The forward foil alone can get us to the island. Just make sure the navigational computer compensates for the damaged aft foil."

Although Quinn tried to sound confident, he wasn't. One more near miss like that and chances were good they'd wind up blasted all over the South China Sea.

16

The second strike team deployed by Aquarius had already made landfall on Shantung Island. The silenced Zodiacs had been beached and the black-clad strikers deployed inland beneath the cover of the dense early-morning mists that hung over the land surface and made unaugmented visual detection difficult.

The house was a former Trappist monastery converted for use as Zhou's personal dwelling. The Prometheus tech found the Spartan atmosphere of the ancient monastery conducive to his work, and he valued the isolation afforded him by the island.

Zhou's personal fortune, derived from his research and development of high-tech munitions systems for China's government-owned arms export bureau, Norinco, allowed him to maintain a private army of security guards.

They came with the ruling Communist Party's blessing. Zhou was too valuable an asset to waste.

DR. LIONEL ZHOU wished he had the eyes of a younger man as he touched the pretty Laotian's cloud of hair, then stroked her smooth cheek.

She had begun by using her hands on which she had rubbed sweetly scented oils. Her supreme mastery of the ancient Shiatzu pressure points, learned from her childhood apprenticeship in Hong Kong's notorious Song houses, was unmatched by any of the others whom he'd employed in recent memory.

Zhou considered himself fortunate to have acquired her services. He felt completely relaxed, soothed, and imbued with a new vitality.

Gently he drew her closer to his body, enjoying the silky feel of her skin against his. Her touch was like a butterfly's, and her lips were warm and velvety. He felt himself responding to her with an ardor that he had only known in his youth. As the Jacuzzi's water swirled around them, his world was reduced to sheer sensations.

THE THREE-MAN Aquarius penetration crew deployed into the strike perimeter silently and swiftly. Black tactical masks made of high-tensile-strength Kevlar, with slits for eyes and mouth, concealed their faces.

The 5.56 mm AUGs in their black-gloved hands were sound-and-flash suppressed. Concentric chamber design incorporated shoot-through baffles to decrease muzzle-flash and report to the barest of minimums.

Each AUG already contained a live round in the pipe and was studded for full-autofire capability.

Death's messengers would strike with a lethal whisper.

With the precise movements of covert professionals the Aquarius terminators scaled the high stone perimeter wall surrounding Zhou's house. The three perimeter guards they encountered at various points on the other side of the wall were taken completely by surprise.

The silenced AUGs wheezed and the sentries were speedily cut down. The dead guards were then dragged from their positions and concealed behind the cover of nearby shrubbery. It was a temporary measure, but it would serve to minimize the risk of detection for the duration of the strike.

The hit team moved on through the low-hanging ground fog, converging on the house. Soon they had reached the main entrance of the converted monastery building. Two more guards, armed with autorifles, stood posts here, oblivious to the slayers who stalked them from the swirling eddies of mist.

Selecting their targets, two of the Aquarius shooters tripped the bolts on their weapons. Blowback took care of the rest.

Barely audible, the next AUG quickbursts claimed the lives of these inner guardians. Shuddering from the impact of the SS109 tumblers, the terminated sentries went down and lay sprawled in twisted heaps as the ground fog crept over their lifeless forms.

The strike leader smiled.

This was a pushover.

Overdependence on manpower and the complete absence of passive IR, long-range TV or laser perimeter alarm sensors had made penetration a simple matter of pumping a few rounds into a few live bodies. He was confident that the remainder of the penetration-and-death strike would be even simpler.

The doors of the house appeared to be made of oak, but intel had confirmed that beneath the wooden veneer lay two inches of high-carbon steel. No problem there, either.

The strike team commander unshipped a prism charge from the musette bag at his waist. The prismatic configuration of the plastic would generate a shaped explosion, funneling the blast energy of the detonating submunition into a precisely delineated zone of high lethality.

He keyed the LED timer on the prism charge for a five-second delay and flattened himself against the wall of the building, well away from the direction of any residual blast effect.

While the commando crew waited for the charge to blow, they stuffed expanding plugs into their ears. Seconds later the heavy steel doors blew inward with a muffled report, the echoes of which quickly faded as the plate steel imploded into petals of ruptured metal under the fierce concussive power of the shaped prism charge.

Even before the acrid blast smoke cleared, the strike leader tossed two black cylinders into the ground-floor level. They were sonic disrupters, which emitted piercing waves of highly disorienting noise.

With the plugs in their ears the Aquarius strikers were protected from the incapacitating effects of the disrupters. But the three guards inside the house weren't prepared and couldn't resist their bodies' urgent dictate. They were caught clapping their hands to their ears as the strike crew darted into the ruptured interior.

Each man swiftly acquired a target as the banshee shriek of the disrupters split the air. The sound-suppressed AUGs wheezed once again, dispensing the verdict of noiseless termination. Three more were added to the mission's body count as the automatic time delay of the disrupters switched off the disabling noise.

Now each of the three Aquarius strikers deployed in search of the individual whose destruction they'd been tasked with carrying out. The house filled with the cadence of combat boots thumping the floor in search of human prey.

One took the stairs onto the balcony that circumscribed the ground floor and began kicking in the doors that fronted the balcony railing. Another sprinted past the stairs into the kitchen behind them and proceeded to search the rooms in the right wing of the house.

The strike leader took the left wing and the rear of the building. He got lucky right away.

He found the Prometheus technician sprawled in his Jacuzzi in the tub room at the back of the house. The old man was partially blind. His eyes were milk-white moonstones in a long face that was ashen with fear.

The pretty Laotian was scrambling to escape through a window when a burst caught her between the shoulder blades. She fell backward and landed across the exercycle behind her, her back arched and her outstretched arms swinging limply.

Though almost completely sightless, Zhou knew precisely what was taking place and understood the desperateness of the situation he was in.

"No!" Zhou cried out at his unseen assailant. "Please. I have money. I will give you—"

A silenced outburst cut short his pathetic pleas and made the old man shudder in the hot tub as the swirling white waters became tinged with curling rivulets of his jetting blood.

"No deal," the killer permitted himself the pleasure of saying, even though there was no longer anybody who could hear it.

His mission accomplished, the Aquarius strike leader had one final task to perform before he and his raiders extracted from the killzone.

He unshipped the trio of black cylinders and armed each high-explosive mine before placing them at triangle points through the tub room. The controlled fragmentation devices were equipped with passive IR triggers that would become operational after an interval configurable by means of a timer touch pad. The antipersonnel submunitions would explode when any newcomers entered the room.

Extracting from the operational perimeter, the Aquarius strike team deployed in reverse, proceeding to retrace their steps toward their beached and camouflaged landing craft. Wary of unforeseen surprises, they kept their combat senses sharp and their AUGs at the ready but encountered no opposition.

Boarding the Zodiacs, the team moved out on the tide to the yacht anchored offshore. The leader of the strike team pulled the black tactical face mask up over his head as he climbed aboard the yacht. He wiped away the sweat that had collected on his brow with the back of his hand and helped the next man over the gunnel.

When the other two members of his team had safely boarded the yacht, the Zodiac was also winched on board. The strike leader looked up at the mission's operation manager, who stood on the bridge and flashed him the thumbs-up.

"Any problems?" the operation manager asked the Aquarius strike team's leader. The point merc recognized the op manager as the operative who was code-named Taurus.

A thin cheroot glowed in Taurus's mouth as he inhaled and then let the smoke swirl out through his nostrils in twin streams. Taurus wasn't taking any more risks with throwaways and screwups, and to make sure of that, he was micromanaging the operation this time around.

"None whatsoever, sir. Everything checked out."

"Okay, good job. There'll be a bonus in it for you. Get your ass below," Taurus barked in response. Then he spun on his heels and strode toward the helmsman in the wheelhouse. Speaking quickly, he issued immediate orders to exit the area of Shantung Island.

As the yacht got under way, Wild Bill Bruckner cast his soulless blue eyes over the island and smiled, flipping the ash from his cigar into the ship's wake as its screws churned the water into a boiling mass.

17

The lead CAT high-speed interceptor craft closed fast on the speeding hydrofoil. While the CAT's prow gunner hammered out withering 7.62 mm minigun autofire, the gunner's mate acquired the *Lao Tzu* in the laser scope of the portable SMAW launcher and let fly the terminally guided round.

The IR-seeking missile went streaking away on a laser-designated trajectory at the *Lao Tzu*. As the warhead exited the launch tube, Quinn saw the computer icon flash to indicate that an ICW was airborne.

Quinn immediately selected the high-performance Vulcan gun as a countermeasure. As soon as Vulcan began chattering out its salvos, Quinn also selected an air-to-surface Exocet missile and targeted the ASCM, antiship capable missile, on the pursuing point craft. Fire from the Vulcan successfully exploded the SMAW round at the apex of its flight trajectory.

Quinn received a kill confirm as the dotted line on his eyes-up display described the course of the Exocet as the ASCM skimmed on a low, radar-evading flight trajectory over the surface of the sea. The flanking CAT craft maneuvered out of the way, but the Exocet's seeker head had obtained a good, solid lock on the CAT's heat signature.

The speedboat's prow gunner swung the minigun from the *Lao Tzu* and now aimed at the ASCM round as the rocket-propelled warhead skimmed over the water on its low angle of elevation attack profile.

With a rush of adrenaline the CAT shooter realized he was unable to acquire the target. The proximity-fuzed Exocet warhead detonated well within the blast radius that would expose the CAT interceptor boat to deadly shrapnel and high-yield explosive shock waves.

The explosion ripped through the hull amidships on the starboard side of the craft. A churning balloon of flame rose over the surface of the water as the CAT was smashed to kindling.

The three mercs on board the craft were killed as the blast effect tore them apart, and a flaming cloud of splintered wreckage rose high into the air before raining down again in small spinning pieces toward the burning surface of the sea.

GOOD KILL, flashed the message on the *Lao Tzu*'s strike management eyes-up display as the icon of the destroyed chase craft blinked out.

That left the point craft and the other surviving flanking craft as contenders Nomad still had to deal with. In the aftermath of the successful Exocet strike neither were taking any chances. They had witnessed firsthand the pure havoc that could be unleashed by the *Lao Tzu*'s sophisticated fire control system.

The leader on board the lead pursuit craft issued orders for all weapons systems to be brought to bear on the *Lao Tzu*. The gunners promptly opened up with their prow-mounted miniguns. SMAW launchers were readied, aimed and fired.

Whizzing steel-jacketed 7.62 mm rounds rotored through the air, the tracers glowing as they struck the *Lao Tzu*'s hull at a cycling rate of six thousand rounds per minute.

The Exocet round having now been expended, Quinn countered this new offensive with more of the Vulcan fire that had been so effective in blowing ICWs out of the air. Vulcan again proved an effective countermeasure, the 20 mm flak front it threw up knocking out the IR-seeking warheads, which all exploded well before they could detonate on target.

As more SMAWs were fired in rapid succession from the two surviving CAT interceptor craft, Quinn clicked on the *Lao Tzu*'s SCLAR capability. The dense-packed multiple launcher was capable of computer-controlled simultaneous or staggered launch of multicaliber rocket rounds. The two SCLAR launchers located to port and starboard of the *Lao Tzu* each carried thirty rocket rounds of various calibers apiece.

As both Vulcan fire and SCLAR rounds met the SMAW warheads in midcourse and took them out, the *Lao Tzu*'s on-board computer allotted the remaining SCLAR rockets to the task of neutralizing the threat of the two remaining CAT pursuit craft still coming on and still throwing minigun fire.

Before the chase crafts could counter with more brilliant rounds, Quinn expended the remaining SCLAR rockets in a phased burst that was locked onto the IR signatures of the two fast-moving CATs.

Although both speedboats began immediate evasive action, the high-explosive warheads fired by Nomad were accurately aimed. Most of them struck their targets with perfect coordination and precision. Twin fireballs merged into a single massive pillar of fire that towered over the surface of the ocean, thundering like an angered sea god disturbed from his eternal sleep.

Obscured by choking black clouds, the remains of the wrecked CATs were completely enveloped in flames. There were no survivors. All Aquarius strike personnel on board the pursuit craft had been wiped out by superior precision-targeted firepower.

Quinn climbed out of the catbird seat and hurried to the prow of the *Lao Tzu*.

Ramsey, at the helm, had been following the progress of the entire firefight via the *Lao Tzu*'s starboard-located long-range TV capability. She looked pleased to see him, then pointed ahead through the windshield at a spot on the horizon. ''What do you make of that?''

Quinn was just able to discern the silhouette of a fast ship already some miles distant from Shantung Island. The vessel was producing a yacht-sized blip on the *Lao Tzu*'s radar.

Ramsey noted by the expression on his face that he didn't like what he saw. There was no apparent reason for the craft to be where it was.

Shantung Island was now only a few thousand feet from their position, and the *Lao Tzu*'s automatic pilot beeped to indicate that the *Lao Tzu* was now being returned to manual steering control.

Taking over the helm, Quinn found the landing easily. Throttling down, he maneuvered the *Lao Tzu* into the slip a few minutes later. Ramsey got out then, and Quinn tossed her the lines, which she made fast to the dock.

Drawing their weapons, Quinn and Ramsey deployed toward the house, which they could now discern beyond the line of jungle foliage at the end of the beach, its upper stories visible from the slightly higher ground on which it stood.

But Shantung Island itself was strangely quiet. The eerie stillness was broken every now and then by the cawing of a bird or the rustling of tropical leaves in the stiff sea wind, but there was no other indication of human habitation. Quinn didn't like the look and feel of the mission environment.

They located the deserted entranceway, inserted Choy's computer key card into the slot, and when the ponderous main gate opened up, they entered beyond the perimeter wall.

A check of the perimeter revealed one of the terminated sentries behind a row of squat shrubbery. Ramsey bent to touch the guard's neck, but Quinn warned her away. He stepped back and hurled a stone onto the center of the dead sentry's stomach. The trembler-switched submunition that had been placed beneath the body, sensitive to the slightest movement, instantly went off, hurling the body into the air.

Quinn and Ramsey moved with renewed caution toward the house. They found the lifeless Zhou in the Jacuzzi, which had already circulated the bloodstained water through its system. The body was jerking back and forth under the power of the circulating water jet, with the head nodding and hands waving in an eerie parody of life created by the mechanical action of the water.

As he stooped to inspect Zhou's remains, Quinn spotted an IR-triggered antipersonnel mine, which distracted him from his scrutiny of what appeared at first glance to be a Chinese ideogram that had been scrawled in blood beside the tub. Reacting quickly, Quinn grabbed Ramsey and pushed her ahead of him toward the doorway.

Together they hit the polished stone floor just as the delayed-action APERS mines detonated, producing a simultaneous shock wave and splinter zone that would have ripped apart any living thing in the tub room caught inside the lethal blast radius. Although Quinn and Ramsey had escaped destruction, any additional clues on or near Zhou's person had been successfully wiped out.

MISSION LOG TWO:

Target

18

The CERT team was being given a run for its money. The virus infecting the Prometheus Network command center's Cray 2010 system had armed the base's STRIKE perimeter defense system.

STRIKE had been conceived as a fail-soft, fault-tolerant umbrella against terrorist attacks, a fully integrated standoff weapons system that was self-implementing and capable of neutralizing a broad spectrum of terrorist offensives.

Software-driven, STRIKE went beyond "smart" or even "brilliant." Artificial intelligence coprocessing gave it the capability of selecting from preprogrammed offensive scenarios, assessing threat levels and automatically initiating counterthreat response by deploying a mix of lethal antipersonnel devices.

Quinn had been instrumental in the STRIKE system's design and had oversight for firms contracted out to manufacture components of STRIKE, which had been built to his exacting specifications.

Because the Prometheus command center's Cray 2010 had turned on STRIKE, the underground complex was now a maze studded with deadly weapons. The core of the system, the Cray's central processing unit at Node Zero was now a dangerous place to be.

Since the CPU was the heart of Prometheus's command center, it was protected by multiple weapon arrays. At the same time the CERT techs needed access to the CPU to perform critical antiviral procedures. It was therefore a matter of urgency to disarm STRIKE, or at least the portion of the system tasked with protecting the Prometheus CPU.

Suiting up in a special rig, one of the CERT technicians was preparing to do precisely that. The suit was actually a sophisticated remote control unit for an advanced-design robotic drone known as a teleoperator.

Every physical motion made by the tech wearing the suit could be translated by telekinetic sensors into identical actions made by a seven-foot robot, hardened against ionizing radiation, explosive blast and highly resistant to splinter-zone antipersonnel ordnance.

Video, passive IR and laser sensors implanted in the robot drone relayed input in a variety of modes by means of a lightweight eye phone rig worn over the technician's head.

As the tech put the drone through its paces, he raised his arm. The drone mimicked his actions. The tech raised a leg, nodded and balled his right hand into a clenched fist. The teleoperator drone followed suit, checking out perfectly.

"Okay, take her in." The tech in the teleoperator rig heard the voice of Jack Redding, the Prometheus command center's director of operations. He was watching from his office overlooking the main operational level of the base, known as the Pit. In Redding's hand was a small commo unit that enabled him to talk to the tech.

Aside from the tech and the drone, the Pit was occupied by only a handful of other personnel. It had been deemed too dangerous to position STRIKE weapons in the vicinity of highest base activity, and so the central control bay was still deemed relatively low-risk.

Nevertheless, there were antipersonnel lasers and nerve gas nozzles that might be activated by the virus at any moment. All personnel in the Pit now worked on a needs-only basis.

"Roger that," Redding heard the tech respond. A moment later the director saw the hulking armored steel drone shamble toward the most dangerous part of the STRIKE system.

The robot was moving into the AKZ, the automated killing zone that was controlled by advanced-design STRIKE weapons, threat sensors and AI-driven computers. The drone's mission was to deactivate the banks of laser weapons, hyperkinetic guns and other defensive systems designed to neutralize terrorist intruders. Primarily intended to deal with human threats, it was hoped that the heavily armored drone could disable STRIKE's most lethal weapons.

With the clank of metal on floor tile the drone shambled into a sterile corridor that looked no different from any of the other passageways linking the various nodes of the command center. It was the only corridor that permitted access to the CPU, and it was designed to put a terrorist strike crew at ease—until it was too late, that is.

Behind the ceiling, deck and walls of the AKZ lurked an array of deadly antipersonnel weapons systems designed to make mincemeat out of any and all intruders. Moments after the drone entered the corridor, the trap was sprung.

Concealed blast doors slid down at either end of the corridor, sealing it off from the rest of the base, trapping the drone inside it as panels in the walls, ceiling and deck retracted to deploy man-killing antipersonnel devices.

Through the video eyes of the drone the tech saw the first of the laser weapons deployed by the AKZ descending from the ceiling just ahead of him. Instantly the tech raised his arms and used his eyeballs to click on the virtual radio button that would send out 7.62 automatic fire from the machine-gun muzzles built into each of the drone's palms.

The tech heard the sound of ratcheting as the rounds let fly at the laser gun just as a beam of red coherent light lanced down toward the drone. The tech's video broke up for a second and then sharpened to focus again, and the tech could see his machine-gun fire shattering the laser cannon as he heard a deafening boom and clouds of thick smoke filled his field of view.

"Nice going," Redding, who had been following the situation on his own eye phones, said into his commo unit. "You sustain any damage?"

"Yeah," the tech answered seconds later. "The drone took a hit in the midsection. I'm having trouble getting it to move."

"Pull out," Redding urgently advised.

"Negative," the tech returned. "The drone's locked in there. Nothing to do but go for broke. I'm—oh, shit!"

Redding and the tech both saw the multiple grenade launcher suddenly pop up from the deck of the AKZ and begin cranking out 40 mm high-explosive rounds. Before the tech could counter, the drone was walloped by successive punches of armor-piercing blast and shrapnel.

There was a sudden flash in both pairs of eye phones, simultaneous with the echoing roar of an explosion before the video link cut out entirely and each eye phone raster went completely blank.

"What the hell happened?" the tech heard Redding shout in his ear beneath a crackle of static.

The tech took it all with good humor. Considering the damage he knew the AKZ was capable of inflicting, the almost fifty-eight seconds that the drone had lasted wasn't too bad an accomplishment.

"Nothing much, except that a ten-million-dollar piece of equipment just got totally trashed."

Just then the blast doors of the sterile corridor slid back into concealed spaces in the ceilings. STRIKE had neutralized the threat and detected no further ones.

Inside the AKZ enormous fans had already blown all traces of toxic blast gases into special filters and retracted all weapons systems into their hidden compartments. And in the center of the sterile corridor lay the shattered and heat-scorched wreckage of the armored robot drone.

WILD BILL BRUCKNER again arrived at the installation that was code-named Castle. As usual, the rogue intelligence operative found himself in awe of the grandeur of the clandestine hardbase. To him Castle symbolized the incarnation of power, the embodiment of Alpha's will to make his vision of global power a reality.

Alpha was awaiting the merc code-named Taurus. He was to be fully briefed on the outcome of the operations thus far.

Although Alpha was shrewd enough to have already checked out everything that had gone down, it was in keeping with his character to be certain that no detail of the operation had been left to chance.

Now Bruckner was going to face Alpha eye to eye. He was one of the few trusted who could come into Alpha's presence.

Bruckner had come to realize that Alpha was a genius with the power to envision the future and see what lesser men couldn't and wouldn't see. A man who was destined to lead the world into a bold, if savage, tomorrow.

Alpha had revealed the existence of a group of minds attuned to a vision of the future in which those who possessed knowledge, wealth and power ruled those who were born to follow.

It was an old vision, and through Daybreak, that vision would soon transform history itself.

About a century before, the Nazi SS had espoused it in a somewhat different form. And at long last some people had recognized a winner's philosophy, and America had absorbed the infrastructure of the Nazi elite, incorporating its genius.

"You may proceed, Taurus," Alpha said as Bruckner entered and prepared himself to brief his leader. "We're most anxious to listen to your report."

19

The chill morning rain lashed Quinn's face as he jogged through the primeval forest. The forest was deep, mysterious and brooding. The rain had begun as a slight drizzle, but had intensified steadily until it became a full-fledged downpour.

Quinn ran until he pushed himself to the limits of physical endurance, determined to persevere until he hit "the wall" if need be and was forced to stop.

The perplexing assignment had drained his mental and physical reserves. Quinn knew he had already hit another kind of wall with the execution of Zhou—the final Prometheus technician, aside from Koenig himself, to remain alive.

Quinn needed to sort out the details, empty himself of all contradictions. He had to find his center, and once there arrive at the essence of the truth.

Pushing his body to the maximum, he kept up a punishing pace, hurling himself forward until his every muscle ached, until he was close to hitting the wall. Quinn would exert every ounce of speed and energy he could muster in order to push out the poisons in his cells and his brain.

The killers had been one step ahead of him and Ramsey all the time. It was almost as if the sinister and mysterious opposition had known their every move in advance.

Quinn was left with only the most tenuous of clues. "Castle" was foremost among these.

Though he had racked his brains and hacked his way into global data-base networks in an attempt to trace the name or reference, Quinn as yet had no inkling as to what Castle could mean.

Was it a place? Did it describe some covert weapons development program? Or was Castle the code name of a clandestine operative? A killer, perhaps, the mastermind behind what he had come to refer to by now as "the Prometheus kills"?

The dogged search through the data bases had yielded nothing to enlighten him. Nowhere was Castle referenced. Yet Quinn believed this fact alone was of high significance.

It was as if someone had gone to extraordinarily great lengths to expunge any mention of Castle. As though someone wanted Castle to remain unknown and invisible. Which could mean that

Castle was something too big or too important to merit even the smallest of leaks.

Yet the Chinese character scrawled in his own blood by Zhou on the floor of the tub room had also turned out to be the ideogram for "Castle." That Zhou had undoubtedly struggled with his last reserves of waning strength to scrawl this single ideogram and no other meant that he attached special significance to it.

What was the meaning of this phraseword? Quinn wondered. What tied it to the murders of the Prometheus techs?

At this stage only Koenig out of all the scientists still remained alive. Quinn sensed that Koenig was the key or *held* the key to the solution of the puzzle that confronted Quinn. Maybe he would discover from Koenig the missing pieces that he needed.

Quinn reached a clearing in the woods from which he had a view of a pine-studded Alpine ridge. He had finally hit his runner's wall. With the rain now beginning to taper off again and the sun coming out, he sat and rested on a big lichen-encrusted boulder.

Suddenly he saw the glint of something reflecting sunlight through a stand of pines between himself and the ridge. He shifted his position, then stood and stared toward where he'd seen the sudden flash. The flash wasn't repeated. Was it the window of a car passing on an autobahn winding through these hills that had caused the flash of light? If that was the case, then why had he noticed no other flashes before or after?

He decided he had to investigate. Though he hadn't counted on any problems during his run, Quinn hadn't gone into the woods unarmed. The lightweight yet lethal Uzi Micro MP was worn behind his back in a breakaway holster. Hidden beneath his sweatshirt, it was instantly accessible from its special Velcro rig.

Suddenly Quinn heard squealing sounds in the distance, and in a while he came upon a wild boar caught in a snare trap, a kind usually set as an antipersonnel device.

Farther on he stumbled upon a small box canyon screened from view by an entrance so narrow that it appeared to be a crevice in the rock face at first glance. Inside the box canyon Quinn found signs of a recent cooking fire. Its occupants had tried to obliterate the spoor but hadn't been successful, either due to inexperience or to haste.

There was enough evidence to indicate to Quinn that somebody had been holed up there, maybe as recently as a half hour before, which would make it at just around the time he had seen the flash of light in the hills.

QUINN RETURNED to Koenig's hunting lodge and showered. Breakfast was now being served in the spacious dining room.

Koenig was already seated at the grand table. Quinn heard his bluff, booming voice and Ramsey's, followed by a burst of laughter as he entered the huge dining room.

The long table was heaped with a bewildering assortment of foods, and the delightful odor of freshly roasted coffee beans wafted from the silver coffeepot.

"There you are, Herr Quinn," Koenig roared, standing to his full height of six feet and beckoning Quinn forward with expansive arm gestures. "You're late. Come, join us. The good food is getting cold."

Quinn sat down at the table opposite Ramsey, while Koenig jovially regarded Quinn with his penetrating gray eyes.

"How was your morning jog?" he asked. "Good? The fresh air, the odor of the pine resin. How I envy you your youth and strength! The mountain air is perfect for the outdoorsman."

"It can certainly be exhilarating," Quinn replied, helping himself to a plate of crisp bacon, "especially when the unexpected happens."

"The unexpected?" Koenig asked, his mouth full of sausage. "How precisely do you mean?"

Quinn told him about his discovery of signs of an encampment in the box canyon. "I thought perhaps you might know something about that?" he concluded. "As I understand it, all of this acreage is your property, isn't it?"

"That is so. And the local people have been poaching on these lands since the days of Frederick the Great," Koenig said, perplexed. "But it is something the security people will want to know about. I will have to remember to inform them. It may even keep them busy enough to give me a moment's peace," he concluded with a laugh.

"You don't have to bother. I already spoke to them."

"Excellent, then we can proceed with other business. Later today, the hunt," Koenig went on. "I have just been telling your charming associate about it."

"Yes," Ramsey put in. "It's quite an old custom. The Bavarians hunt boar at this time every year. It's an almost sacred harvest festival."

"Ah, yes," Koenig said. "And at the end we roast the meat. I am sure you will enjoy it."

THAT AFTERNOON the hunt began. The hunting party drove into a section of woods where herds of wild razorback hogs roamed wild, and they climbed out of the four-wheel-drive vehicles that had brought them and entered the thick pine forest.

Since no conventions dictated the correct weapon to use, each member of the party chose their own. Koenig carried an old pump-action shotgun. Ramsey was outfitted with a Remington rifle mounted with a glass scope.

Quinn's weapon was a .357 Colt Python, also equipped with a scope. He had hunted boar with a handgun before in the Virginia panhandle and enjoyed using that particular weapon against that particular type of game animal.

As the hunters spread out, Koenig took Quinn aside. The trackers had gone on ahead to scout out the game. His eyes darted uneasily from side to side, as if trying to establish that they were alone.

"There are things you don't know about Prometheus," he told Quinn. "Matters I think you should be informed about."

"Such as what?" Quinn asked.

Koenig waved his hand in the air. "Later. After the hunt, we will talk."

Quinn decided to try a shot in the dark. "Castle," he told Koenig. "What's it got to do with Prometheus?"

Koenig's eyes widened as he stared at Quinn. His face went ashen and his lips trembled. "Where did you hear that word? What do you know about Castle?"

"Nothing yet. I was hoping you might be able to enlighten me."

"Castle should have been dismantled years ago," Koenig said with a strange light in his eyes. "The fools should have—"

Just then one of the trackers shouted that they had sighted a herd of razorbacks. Before Koenig could utter another word the hunters were readying their weapons as they confronted the herd.

Quinn caught sight of the first of the boars charging through a break in the underbrush. The animal's eyes were small and piglike, the hide reddish, and fearsome-looking tusks protruded from its curled underlips.

Koenig was fast and agile. All traces of the shock that had seemed to grip him moments before vanished as he brought his shotgun into play and started cutting loose with a load of double-aught buckshot before any of the other members of the hunting party could fire.

The edge of the fan of buckshot caught the boar just behind the right shoulder, opening up an ugly ragged red gash. It was a big razorback, and it turned tail immediately and went squealing off into the woods as the others scattered to all corners. Koenig tried to finish it off, but the boar disappeared into the brush before he could draw a second bead.

As Koenig charged after the boar, Quinn found himself facing off against the biggest razorback of them all. The boar either felt it was cornered or wanted to stand and fight.

The animal snorted, pawed the earth and then charged Quinn with its head down and its hooked yellow tusks in striking position. The enraged game attacked with surprising speed for so ungainly-looking a beast. Quinn knew full well that those tusks were easily capable of disemboweling him if he gave the boar half the chance to strike him in a vulnerable point. Raising the Python and sighting through the scope, he unleashed round after round of hollowpoint slugs.

The slugs all hit their marks. The first one came pounding in low on the boar's back, tearing a bloody red hole in its side. But the .357 Magnum rounds didn't slow the razorback boar down. As more Magnum slugs impacted, the boar swerved to one side but still kept right on coming.

Quinn's final shot was a head shot, and in a flash of crimson the game animal's head snapped back with the impact. The mortally wounded creature let out a bloodcurdling squeal, and its hoofed feet went out from under it.

The heavy carcass fell down with a crash into the underbrush, staining the foliage with its dark blood. The dying boar breathed spasmodically for a few moments, then finally went still.

By the time twilight fell the party had bagged several wild boars. All the razorbacks were large, and the one killed by Quinn—the largest of them all—had apparently been their leader. Its time-yellowed tusks were long and keenly honed from constant sharpening.

Back at Koenig's lodge, mammoth braziers standing on high wrought-iron stanchions were lit against the encroaching chill of evening in the high Alpine mountains as the game was laid out on beds of branches and leaves. The bonfires roared as Koenig, wearing the cockaded Tyrolean hat of the Master of the Hunt, strode forth to make a speech to his guests, an old Junker custom dating back to the days of Germany's feudal barons.

Quinn watched the members of Koenig's household stare at him transfixedly as Koenig began to speak, praising the hunters and reminding them that their efforts had helped thin the herds of game and worked in harmony with the forces that maintained the balance of nature.

When Koenig finished speaking, the members of the hunting party and his household staff raised their hands in polite applause to the great man as he stood limned in the deep copper glow of the fires. Suddenly Koenig's smile left his face. His gray eyes bugged outward. When he opened his mouth, a plume of bright blood spewed from it. Koenig clutched at his throat and pitched forward, landing face first atop one of the boar carcasses. Then, as he lay between the burning torches, fierce convulsions shook his body.

The cause of death was no mystery. It was the steel bolt that a hidden assassin had fired into the side of his neck.

20

By the time Koenig's staff reached his side, the man was already dead. He had died as mysteriously and as inexplicably as the other terminated scientists.

While all eyes were focused on Koenig, Quinn cast his glance elsewhere. He turned toward the perimeter of the hunting lodge, toward the dark pine forest that brooded at its fringes.

For an instant Quinn thought he detected movement amid the trees off to his left. In the smoke-tinged gloaming of deepening twilight visibility was poor, and Quinn couldn't be certain of what he had actually witnessed. He decided to have himself a closer look.

Telling Ramsey to keep watch on the proceedings at the lodge, Quinn drew his Uzi SMG and walked toward the edge of the woods. Penetrating the line of ancient firs, he stopped and scanned the surrounding forest.

Up ahead.

For a fleeting instant a shadowy form was visible in the gloaming. The stocky figure wore black and in a concealed position would be virtually invisible, but when he moved from cover he revealed himself.

The Uzi clutched in his fist, Quinn took off after the running man. He knew he was being drawn deeper into the dark woods—perhaps deliberately so—but there was no other way to play it. Quinn had to count on the likelihood that the shooter's role had been to kill Koenig and extract from the strike zone, and not to draw him into a trap, as well.

A few hundred feet into the woods the black-clad figure suddenly turned, and Quinn knew he was already whipping a concealed weapon into assault position. Anticipating the coming auto-fire salvo, Quinn broke sideways behind the protection of a granite overhang.

Almost simultaneously with Quinn's sideward break, stuttering fire twinkled at the black figure's hip level.

Quinn heard ricochets whine as the bullets spanged off a jumbled heap of boulders nearby. He edged laterally and came up at the far end of the overhang, fisting the compact SMG in a two-handed shooter's stance, ready to throw answering fire at the terminator.

His eyes probing the area for the least sign of movement, his senses on full alert, Quinn whipped the Uzi back and forth, seeking target acquisition. But the shooter had already dropped out of sight. The forest was deserted and silent in the gathering darkness.

Continuing to clutch the Uzi in a two-handed combat grip, Quinn treaded cautiously through the trees, trying to pick up the running man's trail. He found signs of it a few hundred paces ahead. Snapped twigs and leaf litter displaced on the forest floor, the textured print of a sneaker heel, all testified to the shooter's passage through the area a few minutes beforehand.

The nature of the spoor also suggested to Quinn that his quarry was panicking. It indicated a man moving too fast to pay adequate attention to standard overland escape and evasion procedure, which called for sanitizing the trail a striker left behind.

The shooter seemed, Quinn thought, like a man in a hurry to get somewhere, perhaps to a place of safety deeper in the black Bavarian woods.

Twilight had by now fully deepened to night. Without benefit of night vision equipment the level of darkness in the ancient pine woods was nearly total. Quinn was forced to judge direction by means of audial cues, had to use his ears instead of his eyes, catching occasional glimpses of his fleeing quarry in the deadly game of hide-and-seek the two of them played.

Now Quinn recognized the route the killer was taking and understood why it had begun to feel familiar. The killer seemed to be leading Quinn back in the direction of the encampment that he had stumbled across during his jog that morning.

Cresting a tree-studded hill with only sparse growth at its exposed stone top, Quinn caught sight of the elusive killer again. The black-garbed striker was silhouetted against a big, just-risen moon as he stood below the hilltop.

Hearing sounds from above, the shooter looked up, and Quinn caught a glimpse of his face. It had a coarse quality to it, with narrow-set eyes, flat nose and a mouth tightened into a grim line. The killer had daubed his face with streaks of black camou paint, and a black watch cap was worn low on his head.

Autofire twinkled from the muzzle of the SMG blaster in the fleeing man's hand as the shooter unfroze and brought his automatic weapon into play. Quinn tucked left behind tree cover and returned fire using a long burst of Parabellum rounds in order to have a better chance of hitting his target.

The man wasn't hit, but the salvo sent him scurrying through the woods below toward the cluster of granite boulders that concealed the small box canyon. Quinn scrambled down the hillside in pursuit of his quarry, losing sight of him as he sprinted into the woods.

Suddenly a scream of agony pierced the night. The scream rose to a lunatic crescendo that echoed off the surrounding hills, then sank down again and finally died.

Quinn reached the foot of the hill and witnessed a horrifying sight that explained the bloodcurdling sound he'd heard. Just ahead his quarry was impaled on the wooden stake of what appeared to be a variation on the Burmese crossbow trap.

In his haste and carelessness he had apparently stumbled into the trip line of one of the bobby traps set by his own backup. The sixteen-inch spike had nailed him right through the heart, and the dead man now sagged like bloody meat hanging from a butcher's hook.

Without warning lightning flashed and lit up the sky. Rain again began to beat down on Quinn and the assassin dangling from the crossbow trap.

Over the increasingly loud patter of the rain Quinn thought he detected the sound of stealthy movement off to his rear. Alarm bells were going off in his mind. He knew he was being stalked by the dead killer's backup.

Quinn spun around, dashing for the cover of a nearby thicket just as a round from a sound-suppressed rifle crashed into the forest floor, kicking up clods of earth around his feet. As Quinn had predicted he would, the shooter's backup had arrived on the scene.

GEMINI HAD OVERSIGHT of the Koenig hit.

The second merc of the two-man hit team deployed by Gemini had been waiting for the shooter in the concealment of the Bavarian night. He was equipped with a nightscope-mounted, sound-suppressed AUG using image-intensification detection apparatus.

Unphased by the weather conditions in the operations zone, the Gemini merc had seen the shooter coming and was ready to interdict and terminate the lone man on his tail. But the shooter had panicked and run right into the booby trap they had set for pursuers. The merc had lost his head in a most unprofessional manner, but he had paid the ultimate failure penalty. Both of them had been well compensated in advance, and the risks went with the territory.

Now Gemini Two acquired Quinn in the scope reticle of his AUG weapon. The green raster image clearly showed Quinn moving at a crouch through the forest. Despite the rain and the cover of the dense brush in which he squatted, electro-optical image intensification showed up the target silhouette with perfect clarity.

No sweat, Gemini Two thought. Easy kill.

With his target framed in the cross hairs, the Gemini backup squeezed off the 5.56 mm round. Quinn felt stone chips sting his cheek as the near-silent round struck a big flat rock nearby. There had been scant muzzle-flash from the sound-suppressed AUG, and Quinn had no true sense of the direction of the attack.

But he knew the sniper was out there, somewhere within the operational limits of the AUG's range. Somewhere close.

Nomad had a good idea of what he was up against, and he had to respect the shooter's ability to take him down. A crack shot with a night-scope firing at him from good cover would have him outgunned for sure.

The Uzi was a handy piece to have in a close-in firefight. Up against a rifle, though, it was no contest. The higher-powered, longer-ranged weapon would shut out an SMG every time.

Lightning flashed again, a big, jagged bolt that lit up the night, exposing the rain-swept boulders and tall trees and the rivulets of water that sluiced through the mud. A few seconds later a deafening clap of thunder rolled through the hills. The epicenter of the storm cell was coming closer. It was almost on him, Quinn thought.

Quinn knew he would have to even the odds if he was to make it out of these deadly hills alive. The storm would help him.

The nightscope the merc was squinting through would be operating at minimum effectiveness during the flashes of lightning. Bloom-out occurred when the sensitive image-intensification apparatus was overexposed to a light source. Even electronic antibloom technology could only do so much to prevent this from happening. It was an inherent design element in image-intensification hardware.

Waiting until the next flash of lightning occurred, Quinn made his move. Breaking from cover while the woods were lit up as brightly as day went against his every instinct, but Quinn forced his brain to override these inhibiting reflexes.

He gambled that despite the brightness of the lightning flash the nightscope mounted on the rifle would be functioning at greatly reduced efficiency. Depending on where he was looking and how fast Quinn acted, the merc could be as good as blind to his movements throughout the few seconds during which the woods were lit up.

He had guessed right, he realized, when he wasn't shot at. Additionally Quinn's fast scan of the area had revealed the suppressor-augmented muzzle of the AUG projecting from some shrubbery a few yards away from his position. As the lightning flickered out and a peal of thunder boomed across the hills, Quinn crouch-walked from the thicket he'd sheltered in.

As Quinn stole up to one side of the gunman, the shooter didn't suspect that Quinn had crossed laterally to his left and was now hidden behind the trunk of a tree on his blind side. Uzi in hand, Quinn picked up a rock and flung it across the shooter's path. Reacting purely on instinct, the killer fired a subdecibel 5.56 mm burst at the tumbling rock. As the man let loose his heat, Quinn broke from cover and hustled toward the shooter's concealed position.

Gemini Two had already realized what was happening and was whipping the business end of the AUG in the direction he suspected the assault would come from. Quinn shot first and caught him on the shoulder and neck with a salvo of 9 mm PB fire from the Uzi before the merc could get off a burst.

The AUG dropped to the ground, and a pulse beat later was followed by the shooter himself. Quinn found Gemini Two sprawled in some bushes with a huge hole in the side of his face. Blood was leaking out of the hole. The burst had sheared away most of the shooter's lower jaw, leaving behind an ugly red mess in its place.

The man was trying to tell him something, Quinn realized, though only dark bubbles of blood came from his frantically working mouth. Quinn quickly understood what the downed man was trying to say. Raising the Uzi with a nod, Quinn fired a mercy round into the pulverized face, releasing the merc forever from his sudden unbearable torment.

Quinn made his way back to the hunting lodge after searching the bodies of the terminated Gemini crew. Like all the other mercs sent by the opposition so far, the clothes they wore turned out to be completely sterile.

Ramsey shook her head as she saw Quinn return to the lodge. Quinn arrived just in time to see them covering Koenig's face with a sheet. Koenig was the final Prometheus scientist to be murdered by faceless, nameless assassins for no apparent reason.

21

Ramsey emerged from the shower with a towel wrapped around her hair. She was otherwise unclothed. Approaching the bed in which Quinn lay, she tossed the towel to the floor and tilted back her head in a motion both sensual and defiant.

Seventeen hours earlier the investigation into the deaths of the Prometheus scientists had run into its final dead end, at least as far as Quinn was concerned, with the death of Wilhelm Koenig.

That Quinn had been tantalizingly close to a breakthrough was an added source of frustration. Just before the unknown assassin had struck, Koenig had intimated to Quinn that there was something of importance he'd wanted to say.

Now Quinn's hope for a breakthrough had ended in a wash. At a briefing earlier that day Quinn and Ramsey had brought Bruckner up to date.

Bruckner had told them in return that the unofficial word now was that despite Koenig's absence from the population count the Prometheus Net was scheduled to go on-line as planned. The world could now only watch and wait as the CERT team at Storm King Mountain worked behind the scenes to purge the malfunctioning computer of viral contamination.

Bruckner had informed Quinn that payment into his numbered Swiss account had already been made. A handshake ended the briefing and Quinn's involvement with Prometheus.

But Ramsey wasn't satisfied with a dispassionate goodbye in a Berlin hotel room. She had demanded a farewell on other terms, however. She made love to Quinn with a passion that wouldn't abate, that only seemed to grow in intensity with each successive climax.

Now she seated herself astride him and began to move with slow deliberate undulations that were reciprocated by Quinn beneath her. Her eyes shut tightly, she felt the heat and pressure building within, to be followed by sudden, sweet release.

It was time to end the game, she thought, as she reached behind her back and unfastened the small hypodermic injector no bigger than the cap of a pen that she had taped to the nape of her neck. It was filled with a fast-acting neurotoxin distilled from shellfish, impossible to detect.

It was time for Genesis to fulfill her contract.

In a fluid, practiced motion Ramsey pressed the blunt nose of the injector against the pulsating vein in Quinn's throat. There was a hiss of pneumatic pressure as the neurotoxin was released into Quinn's bloodstream. She felt his body stiffen and saw his eyes bulge in his head.

Genesis knew there would be no struggle. The poison acted almost instantaneously.

Ramsey uncoupled herself as Quinn arched his back in a final spasm, then collapsed back down onto the bed. She stood and watched him, the injector still clutched in her hand. Bending over Quinn's body, she placed her ear to his chest. There was still a faint heartbeat but that would fade soon, too, she knew.

Still naked, Ramsey went to her purse and removed the SIG-Sauer semiautomatic pistol and the silencer from it. Threading the silencer into the barrel, she snapped a round into the chamber and aimed the business end of the weapon at Quinn's face.

She didn't want to complete the act of murder in this way, but tradecraft called for her to confirm the kill.

She knew she had to.

Ramsey's finger tightened on the trigger of the SIG, but she couldn't make herself squeeze it past the breakpoint. A look of amazement crossed her face.

This had never happened before.

Genesis had seduced her other victims in this way and had always carried out the assigned termination directive. There had never been any question that she would fail, either in her own mind or in the minds of her paymasters.

She had walked the Stations of the Cross at Taranto and was certain that she'd been purged of the weakness that had afflicted her after the last contract termination. She had believed she had made peace with herself and would be able to continue killing without suffering conscience, without feeling remorse.

The ordeal at Taranto had never failed to empty her psyche of guilt or bolster her resolve to continue the deadly game.

Yet it had now.

There had been feelings for some of the black widow's prior kills, but emotion had never entered into the equation before. Sex had always been a part of the web that Genesis had spun to ensnare her victims, and at the center of that web of pleasure, at the precise moment of release, she had exposed her stinger and struck.

Ramsey took a deep breath as she had been trained to do, reaimed the SIG and tried once more to squeeze off the round into the immobilized man's face. The weapon shook in her trembling hand. Her finger tightened on the trigger but again wouldn't squeeze past the breakpoint. Genesis was still unable to complete the task of termination.

Ramsey realized in the end that she couldn't. She dressed quickly and put the spent injector and the again broken-down pistol into her purse.

Quinn was a goner, anyway. The neurotoxin alone would do the job, no question about that.

She glanced once more at Quinn's motionless form prostrate on the bed, picked up the telephone and punched in the number at which her case officer waited to receive confirmation of the kill.

"It's done," she said the moment the line picked up.

"You know the meeting place. Meet me there in twenty minutes."

Replacing the handset on the cradle, Ramsey left the room without daring to look back at Quinn's still form.

COLD BLACK RAIN FELL in twisting sheets as the cab stopped on a deserted street in the Berlin warehouse district.

The taxi driver was perplexed. "Are you sure this is the place you want?" he asked the woman in the back seat.

She didn't reply except to hand over her fare and a tip, then exited the car. The driver thanked her and drove away with a shrug. His business, after all, was to take fares to their destinations, not to ask questions.

Ramsey turned and walked through the pelting rain. The place she would meet her control was several blocks from the spot where she had been let off, and she hurried there against the bad weather.

When she reached the warehouse, she let herself in, punching in the access code and hearing the metal bar in the door snap back. A flash of lightning cast dingy gray light through the high casement windows set in the upper story of the warehouse and illuminated the solitary figure who stood on the catwalk that wound around the window line. He was leaning on the railing, looking down into the interior of the warehouse.

"Stay where you are," he called down. "I'll be right there."

Moments later she heard the whining of the lift that brought Bruckner down to her level. Another lightning bolt lit up the slowly descending steel cage, illuminating the face and form of Bruckner.

"You look like hell, babe," he said as he let himself out of the cage and walked toward her, footsteps echoing on the pavement.

"I carried out your directive. That's all you need to know. Now pay me, Taurus, and let me get out of here."

Bruckner smiled and reached into his pocket. Instead of an envelope he withdrew a small silenced .38-caliber Walther and pointed the pistol at Ramsey's face. "I don't think so," he said, shaking his head. "With Quinn taken care of and the Prometheus scientists out of the picture, you're no longer an asset. In fact," he went on, "you're a distinct liability, babycakes."

"Put the gun away. You don't have the authority."

Her eyes steady on his, she was reaching into the pocket of her raincoat where a .24-caliber backup piece was nestled. Her fingers closed around the handgrip as she prepared to jerk it into play.

Bruckner's face went dead, and his fingers closed around her arm, tightening like steel coils.

"Don't try it," he snarled, shoving the sound-suppressed muzzle of the .38 against her temple and cocking the hammer of the double-action weapon. "Don't even think of it." Holding the .38 on her, Bruckner reached into her pocket and came up holding the .25.

"You're bluffing, Taurus," she snapped. "I repeat, you don't have the authority to terminate. You and I are run by the same man." With her other hand she pulled a spring-loaded knife from concealment within her coat sleeve.

Bruckner laughed. It wasn't a pleasant sound. "If you're thinking about Alpha, forget it. I, and I alone, answer to Alpha. You were Alpha's whore, nothing more. You were never anything but a tool to be used by him. To coin a phrase, babe, you were expendable. Still, maybe you do have a use or two left in you at that," Bruckner concluded with a snort of depraved laughter.

He reached out quickly, his hand a white blur. There was a tearing sound as Ramsey's dress was torn, exposing pink flesh.

She moved just as quickly, snapping open the spring-loaded knife and bringing it up in a vicious swipe at Bruckner's heart. Bruckner was half expecting the move, though, and he was ready. Sidestepping the thrust, he brought the base of the

Walther's handgrip down on her wrist with crushing force.

"That was dumb," he told her as the knife clattered to the concrete deck. "Now I'll make you wish I'd killed you right away. In the end you'll beg me, bitch. That's a promise."

Suddenly he lashed out with the flat of the gun against her temple and knocked her to the concrete floor of the warehouse. She groaned, fighting to keep from blacking out but already beginning to lose the battle.

Bruckner put the gun away and began fiddling with his belt buckle as he swayed over her. The sound of thunder roared in his ears, and a dull, glazed-over light kindled in his soulless blue eyes.

22

The roaring of blood in his ears kept Bruckner from hearing trouble coming his way. Without warning he was grabbed from behind and spun quickly around by powerful hands. Now he was looking straight into the grinning face of a dead man.

"Quinn!" he shouted. "How the hell did you—"

The rest of his sentence never got spoken. Quinn smiled menacingly and hauled off with a punishing right straight from the shoulder that drowned his words in a bloody froth.

The clenched fist smashed into Bruckner's face with piledriving force. His nose burst apart under the impact of the blow, and blood began spraying.

Knocked back on his heels, Bruckner flung out his arms like a scarecrow. He collapsed to the concrete in a floundering heap and lay there, pie-eyed. Regaining his wits, he managed to rise to a sitting position, propping himself on his hands as blood gushed out of his nose and ran down his shirt.

Looking up, he saw the room spin in a kaleidoscopic array of multiple images. From the center of the spinning tunnel four Quinns were lumbering toward him. Every one of the Quinns had a forbidding look on his face.

Bruckner managed to reach inside his jacket and whip the Walther .38 autopistol from shoulder leather. His draw seemed slow and jittery, but it was fast enough. The black-framed 9 mm PB firearm was already emerging from its nesting place inside his black leather pit holster as Quinn moved in.

Quinn had expected Bruckner to reach for heat, though, and was prepared to deal with the contingency. Countering the pistol draw with an accurately delivered hwa rang do toe kick, Quinn knocked the silenced weapon from Bruckner's grasp. The Walther went skittering across the concrete floor of the warehouse and stopped with a muffled thud somewhere in the shadows.

Bruckner bellowed, pushing himself up off his feet with manic strength borne of rage and defiance. Tucking his head down, he charged Quinn.

Quinn sidestepped the wild charge, but Bruckner's adrenaline level achieved what his reflexes and fighting skill alone had been unable to. The big man's shoulder grazed Quinn's rib cage with enough steam behind it to send him reeling. Bruckner managed to grab hold of Quinn in the process, and both of them were sent sprawling to the hard concrete deck of the warehouse by the momentum of their collision.

Thrashing and rolling on the floor, each man struggled to gain supremacy over the other, lashing out with hand blows and kicks in a furious contest. In the course of the free-for-all, Bruckner got lucky with a finger jab he managed to get into Quinn's eyes.

Quinn saw stars explode and reflexively relaxed his grasp on his adversary's windpipe. With Quinn momentarily blinded, Bruckner scrambled erect.

He cast about for a weapon and spotted a steel crowbar lying on the floor near a heap of wooden packing crates. Scrabbling for the crowbar, he grasped the weapon securely in both hands and swung it viciously down at Quinn's head.

Rolling aside at the last possible instant, Quinn still caught part of the pulverizing blow on the fleshy part of his right shoulder. A ball of flame spread throbbing waves of pain down his arm and the right side of his chest. Again Bruckner raised the heavy crowbar, this time to deliver the stopper from high overhead.

Quinn lashed out with the sole of his foot and caught his opponent squarely in the groin. Bruckner let out a howl of agony as a bolt of lightning speared through his nervous system.

Bellowing like a wounded ram, Bruckner let go of the steel rod, which dropped to the floor with a dull clang. He sank to his knees, clutching his badly injured testicles. Then he staggered to his feet and dodged out of sight, cursing and yelling in pain. Wincing from his own injuries as he rose to his feet, Quinn drew his Uzi from shoulder holster and doubled back to check on Ramsey before going after Bruckner.

The woman was slowly recovering, but she had a nasty lump on her head the size of a robin's egg. Quinn felt that he didn't owe her anything after she'd tried to kill him, but he hoped to get some answers from her, so he helped her behind some crates and told her to stay put. Then he took off in search of Bruckner.

By this time the rogue agent had reached the steel weapons locker he kept at the warehouse in preparation for unforeseen contingencies. He had decided to deal with Quinn the no-risk way—shut him up for good.

Casting backward glances, sweat beading his florid face, the spook terminator fumbled with the combination on the lock. Then there was a beep and the lock sprang open. Bruckner reached inside the gun safe and closed his hands around the advanced-design hardware he'd cached there.

Working quickly, he crammed spare ammo clips into his pockets and hefted the lightweight black bullpup-configured weapon from the rack inside the gun safe. He was already starting to feel a whole lot better as he snapped a fresh clip of ammo into the bullpup's receiver and chambered the first round by retracting the bullpup's cocking lever.

Next he clicked on the laser designator that was secured by clamps to the bullpup's receiver frame. A thin pencil line of ruby light immediately issued from the scope.

Bruckner moved the bullpup back and forth, watching the ruler-straight laser beam trace a crimson line across the crates and walls of the warehouse storage area. Now Quinn would have a surprise coming. The weapon was loaded with some special ordnance, a kind that would pay the bastard back the way he deserved.

With the bullpup locked and loaded with its unconventional ammo, Bruckner spun on his heels and headed for the entrance to the room. Suddenly he saw Quinn dart into view, illuminated by a flash of lightning streaming in through a warehouse skylight.

Bruckner laughed a madman's laugh as he raised the bullpup to chest height and sighted the thin bloodred beam on the running man's chest, then squeezed off a burst in Quinn's direction. The spook felt the bullpup buck in his fists, and he heard the faint metallic sound of the blowback-driven rounds as they whizzed out the muzzle of the weapon.

No brass was expelled because the bullpup fired caseless ammo. There was little sound either except for the faint *pfitt* of the rounds ejecting and the thud of the impact into the opposite wall. Otherwise the weapon was completely silent.

No muss, no fuss. Just sheer, murderous hell.

"Good thing I wasn't trying to hit you, Quinn," Bruckner shouted as Quinn broke for cover, scrambling behind some empty steel drums. "If I did, you'd be cat chow by now, kemo sabe."

Bruckner laughed and stepped confidently into the open. The crimson pencil line of the laser target designator beam lanced out into the shadows like the probing antenna of a poisonous monster wasp.

"This here's the latest and the greatest. Fires flechettes made from the same depleted uranium rods they use in tank ammo. Hyperkinetic rounds, bucko. They pack a mean fuckin' wallop."

The gleaming ruby beam of the laser designator came to rest on one of the big crates at the other end of the room. Bruckner aimed the bullpup and fired another multiround burst of flechette ammo into the crate. The inch-long depleted uranium kinetic energy needles ripped through the crate, reducing it to a pulverized cloud of wood.

"Just think what this little honey of a weapon'll do to your worthless hide, good buddy," Bruckner cackled gleefully. "Just think about it. For the next few seconds you got to live. You think real hard about it!"

The ruby light of the laser spotter scope skittered across more crates and came to rest on the empty fuel drum behind which Quinn had dodged.

As Bruckner's index finger jerked the bullpup's trigger, Quinn broke from cover, snapping a burst of Uzi fire at his spook opponent. Bruckner jerked backward in reflex action just as his finger passed the breakpoint.

The whizzing burst of flechette rounds followed the beam of the laser and slammed into the metal drum. The force of impact created terrific stresses on the metal of the drum, causing it to explode as if the flechettes had been tipped with explosive warheads.

Lethal shrapnel razored through the air as Quinn tucked left and rolled to the safety of a ceiling-high stack of wooden crates, snapped off another burst of 9 mm Uzi PBs and got through the door.

Bruckner recovered his balance and launched another flechette burst, chewing up the side of the doorway but failing to hit his intended mark. Ejecting the spent clip and snapping in a fresh magazine he pulled from his pocket, Bruckner again went after his quarry.

Quinn's Uzi had run dry by now, and he was fresh out of reloads. Just then he spotted a stack of old aluminum signs lying in a dusty corner. As he rushed toward them, he devised a desperate gambit to survive the shoot-out.

From the room beyond, the shaft of ruby light was walking toward him with jittering, psychotic movements. It was seeking him, sniffing him out, and when it found him, it would give him away to the man who wielded the deadly gun.

Quinn wheeled around a heartbeat before the laser beam touched his shoulder. In both hands he clutched one of the signs he had taken from the stack, its bare aluminum reverse side turned toward Bruckner.

Bruckner screamed as the ruby laser radiation bounced off the reflective back of the sign and struck him squarely in the face. Now he was temporarily blinded by the designator beam of his own weapon.

With his eyes on fire he pumped the trigger of the bullpup in a homicidal fury, sweeping the barrel around in a desperate attempt to hit his unseen target. The blind fire wasn't accurate, but it served some purpose: Quinn was forced to keep his head tucked down.

A single good strike, even a ricochet from a partially spent flechette round, could literally tear him to pieces. The kinetic energy that the deadly needles transferred to anything they hit would shatter him as if he were made of plaster.

Quinn had no choice but to hunker down behind the cover of a metal dumpster as Bruckner fired the weapon in a wild frenzy of hatred, then reloaded and discharged another clip.

Fortunately Bruckner was nearly blind, and his only concern at that point was to stage a getaway as quickly as possible. He would deal with Quinn another day. Before his weapon ran dry he was beating a path toward a fire door that led to the rain-swept street where his wheels were parked.

Quinn heard the sound of a powerful car engine revving from the street outside. Rushing to the swinging exit door, he saw the small compact car accelerate from the curb and career back and forth on the rain-slicked asphalt before rounding a corner. Then Bruckner was gone into the night, and Quinn knew that he, too, would have some unfinished business to transact.

Ramsey had found her gun and was holding it in a two-handed firing stance as Quinn approached her. She stared at him with wild, frightened eyes as the automatic pistol shook in her trembling hands.

"You don't need that anymore," Quinn told her, reaching to take away the gun.

Parked in a geosynchronous orbit two hundred miles above the surface of the earth, the phased-array network of the Prometheus energy satellites gleamed in the light of the distant sun. Four giant mylar radiation collectors extended outward from the central core of each satellite. Each solar collection panel contained thousands of individual photovoltaic panels and was tethered to the main unit by fifty-foot-long umbilicals.

Inside the main unit of each satellite, a small yet powerful nuclear reactor generated millions of volts of electrical current from the harnessed energy of the sun. The electrical power was then converted to microwave energy and beamed down via the dish antenna situated at the center of each satellite to a complex of collection stations based around the earth.

Girdling the globe, Prometheus promised to yield a virtually limitless supply of cheap energy to mankind as soon as the network went on-line. The world awaited the moment when the ambitious program would finally provide it with an alternative to fossil fuels and dangerous nuclear power stations.

But on the earth below, in the tunnel complex within Storm King Mountain where the Cray 2010 command-and-control computer that governed Prometheus was located, optimism was low while anxiety ran high.

The command center was situated at the heart of an underground installation that stretched for many hundreds of feet through the mountain in a labyrinthine maze of immense burrows drilled and blasted into the heart of the stony-iron core.

After a massive feasibility study, Storm King had been selected to house the command center because its rock contained a high percentage of ferrous ore, hardening it naturally against the threat of electromagnetic pulses that were released by nuclear explosions and were lethal to all forms of electronic equipment. Nuclear terrorism, acts of war or Chernobyl-type disaster scenarios couldn't affect the vital role of the Prometheus Net.

The layout of Prometheus's nerve center, its ready room, resembled that of an amphitheater, with tiers of telemetry console stations arranged in a series of concentric circles that spiraled downward to a central bank nicknamed the Pit by the technicians who worked down there. Command, control and communications consoles requiring the highest security clearances made up the central ring of the control center with the outer tiers—each built one level above the next—devoted to progressively lower-level functions and backup systems telemetry.

Occupying most of one hemispherical wall of the ready room was a patchwork of giant digital view screens on which could be seen ever-changing computer-generated maps of the earth showing the Prometheus orbits overlaid on the globe, real-time video of the spaceborne enersats and other constantly updated data. One of the screens was now tuned to WNN, the World News Network, which was broadcasting the funeral services taking place in Germany for Wilhelm Koenig, the man who had devoted his life single-handedly to turning Prometheus from a dream into a reality.

Many illustrious dignitaries attended the funeral, including the President of the United States. Thus far a combined effort by global intelligence agencies had managed to keep the truth about Koenig's manner of death a secret.

The world believed that Koenig had succumbed to a sudden stroke during a hunting party at his mountain estate. Much like the other Prometheus kills, Koenig had died a martyr to the cause he had championed throughout his entire life.

Directly across the vast bunker housing the nerve center's computer consoles, glass-paneled observation rooms and administrative offices looked out on the view screens and the proceedings in the Pit below.

The office of Jack Redding, the command center's director of operations, was situated in one of those glass-paneled rooms.

A man of medium height with steel-gray hair, Redding had been a natural choice to head the command center. For years he had been czar of the U.S. Department of Energy and had been instrumental in convincing the President to support Koenig's Prometheus initiative in the 1990s.

Now, precisely an hour and fifteen minutes after being awakened by his deputy's call from a much-needed sleep break, the command center director stood holding a mug of steaming black coffee as he watched the furious activity below. Redding then turned and looked back toward the key members of his staff who were seated at the conference table in the room.

Their faces were drawn and grim. Redding realized that his must certainly look that way, too. It would have to if it mirrored the chagrin he felt at the multiple blows that had just sent the program reeling.

The problems with the Cray had been bad enough, but now that Wilhelm Koenig—the human symbol of the Prometheus Project—had been killed, he wondered if the program could survive the setback. For a fleeting instant he caught sight of his face reflected in the glass of his office window. With a shock he saw the hollow eyes and gaunt cheeks, evidence of the tremendous strain he was under.

After many days of wrestling with the destructive worm that had infected Prometheus's computer, the CERT experts still couldn't state with any degree of certainty how much of the malicious program they had purged from the system. Redding's most recent intel was that the virus's front end—the so-called user interface or program shell that the virus hid behind—was a launch vector stabilization code written for the Cray by a Silicon Valley consulting firm.

When the FBI came calling at the firm's last known address, they found that no such business had ever occupied the Laundromat and bar located at the site. Nor did the audit trail lead anywhere, either. Every supplier of software programs had checked out clean.

But the infected software was anything but clean. It was a breeding ground for system-crashing bugs that were too fast and too smart for the world's best minds to deal with so far.

Some of the CERT techs believed it was only the software that had been infected with the bugs, but others claimed that the hardware, too, had been infected, and the virus had hidden parts of itself inside the microchips that comprised the Cray 2010's silicon brain, ready to replicate themselves and infect any new software program that was transferred into the system.

To fine-tune the parameters of the situation was one of the purposes of the present crisis-asessment meeting. Another purpose was to determine if the CERT team could even arrive at a conclusion as to how to proceed.

The declared deadline for announcing the on-line status of the Prometheus Net was quickly approaching. In another seventy-two hours the President of the United States, in place of Wilhelm Koenig, was scheduled to announce at a special session of the United Nations that the Prometheus Net was fully operational.

But right now every person in Redding's office could watch the big screen on the other side of the Pit and see the President at Wilhelm Koenig's final rites in Berlin. Koenig was awarded the solemn honors due Germany's greatest modern hero, a man whose vision of the future had redeemed his country in the eyes of many from its sins in the course of the Second World War.

Redding turned back to the CERT team and the members of his staff. "People," he said, "I know I'm asking you to make a tough call. But it's necessary. The *Challenger* disaster in the eighties hamstrung America's space program. The National Space Telescope was a boondoggle for NASA in the nineties. The Mars mission of 1997 almost killed the exploration of outer space. I don't have to remind you of that nightmare."

Redding didn't have to say anything more. Many of the men and women seated at the conference table had been directly associated with the U.S.-Russian effort to put a team of astronauts on Mars.

Every one of them winced involuntarily at memories of the video images of the Mars probe spacecraft smashing against the enormous nickel-iron asteroid that had come out of nowhere, a big space rock whose orbit had been too erratic for the mission's course computers to track or predict.

"I don't have to tell you that Prometheus is of potentially greater importance to humanity than any space mission yet launched," Redding went on. "Not only will a disaster threaten to doom the world's space exploration efforts for the rest of the century, but it'll deprive developing nations of immediate benefits. Prometheus can transform the world. We must be damn sure of our options."

One by one the CERT specialists delivered their reports. The first to be heard from stated that, in his view, enough of the computer virus had been purged from the Cray 2010 computer to permit partial energizing of the satellite system.

Another technician immediately jumped to his feet to contest this assertion. His claim was that the computer virus was far too unpredictable for any claims to be made at this stage. He could say that the invading code was mostly a "worm," a rogue program that slithered through the system, making copies of itself as it went along to spread the infection further.

"The problem with a worm," the technician continued, "is integral to the software that runs the Prometheus computer itself, which uses what we call 'knowbots' to function."

"I'm somewhat familiar with the concept," Redding said with a nod.

During the SDI or Star Wars research of the eighties and nineties, software programs weren't fast enough to detect incoming warheads with any degree of accuracy. Something more was needed and was eventually developed by turning an adversity into an advantage.

"The knowbot concept came about as a direct result of some of the most deadly computer viruses known," Redding concluded.

"Correct," another CERT member put in. "Specifically the Pakistani Brain Virus and the SCORES viruses. At any rate, the idea was to create benign virus programs that did exactly what the destructive viruses did, which was to run in the background and handle specific tasks on their own without the intervention of the main program. This speeded up operations to the extent where space-based lasers could and did function within acceptable performance parameters."

"Okay," Redding assented, "but I still don't get your point."

"The point is," the first CERT man who had spoken said, "that the Prometheus virus isn't really a virus at all. It is, in fact, something entirely new because it corrupts the operation of the knowbots and not the main program per se." The speaker paused and looked searchingly into the faces of every member of the CERT panel convened in his office. "I think everyone here comprehends what I'm saying."

"Yes," Redding exclaimed. "It's not a virus anymore, is it? It's more like a computer cancer." Redding nodded to himself and picked up the handset of the phone on his desk. "I'm informing the President," he said, his haggard face now grim. "I'm going to recommend that the activation of the Prometheus Net be put on hold and the computer destroyed."

MISSION LOG THREE:

Kill

24

Quinn was hunched over the video display terminal. Shifting patterns of colored light traversed his tense features as he punched in sequence after coded sequence at the keypad.

The object of this exercise was one of singular importance. Quinn was to break into the Prometheus task-force computer system linked to the National Security Council's covert data retrieval system. Only in this top-secret data base could Quinn hope to uncover the significance of the mysterious "Castle" that now seemed central to cracking the case.

Although the NSC DBMS had been among the first he'd searched because of its relationship to Prometheus, Quinn hadn't suspected that the data base was only the "front end" of a covert information storage-and-retrieval system. Purely by chance he had decided to try it once again and had stumbled on the electronic "back door" that was a portal into the covert DBMS.

As he worked, he recalled his conversation with Ramsey about the nature of the code name Castle. "Was Castle a place?" he had asked her.

"Yes," she had answered. "It's a place. I've been there. But I don't know where it is."

"Why not?"

"Bruckner always took precautions. I was put into a semidrugged state when I was taken there. One minute I'm getting into a car to head for the airport, and the next thing I know I'm there."

"With the one they call 'Alpha'?"

"Right," she had answered, turning away. "He did...things with me. He was unlike anyone else. Other men might use a woman's body. Alpha, he takes your mind, rips out your soul."

"And you never really saw him? You never heard his voice?"

"No. Alpha was cloaked electronically whenever I was with him. He once said it was some kind of neural disrupter chip under his skin. It distorted visual and audial perception of his face and voice." She shivered involuntarily. "When I think of how that bastard used me..."

"He's used us all," Quinn had said. "Now it's our turn to get even with the dirtbag."

Bruckner, too, had used them both. Bruckner and the mystery man called Alpha. After the deadly turnaround play at the Berlin warehouse, Quinn realized that the spook free-lancer had run a classic "false flag" operation on him, sent him on his mission as a stalking-horse.

The way the operation had been designed, it was Quinn himself who had set up the remaining Prometheus scientists for the kill. He had flushed them out of hiding, drawn them into the open for the strike teams to knock them down and been expertly distracted from suspecting the truth by repeated hit attempts directed against him.

Bruckner had turned Quinn into his cutout.

Ramsey had been Bruckner's insurance policy, Quinn surmised. She was the spook's way of making certain every loose end was tied up. Bruckner himself had tried to tie up the final loose end by taking care of Ramsey after he had issued her the termination directive on Quinn.

Quinn had suspected Ramsey early on. He had found himself in what former CIA director Stansfield Turner had once called "a wilderness of mirrors."

Quinn hadn't known when or how it would go down, but he knew that a put-away hit was in the offing, and he also knew Ramsey was the logical candidate to do the deed.

But he had needed to be certain. In case Ramsey were to use poison he had shot himself full of a broad-spectrum antidote specific to neurotoxins. This had been a calculated risk, but he had figured that only the fastest acting neurotoxin serum would be the weapon of choice.

Quinn had gambled correctly but had almost paid the ultimate price despite his preparedness. The highly active shellfish neurotoxin she had injected into his neck had, in fact, almost killed him.

Prometheus was only part of the picture, though, Quinn was sure. If the energy satellite network were sabotaged, what then? Who would stand to benefit most from it?

There had to be another dimension to the entire equation, some factor Quinn didn't yet grasp, something tied in with Prometheus and that required the silencing of all the technicians who had worked on designing and building the system.

Castle was the key to determining the nature of that missing link as well as the identity of the individual at the center of the web, the unseen mover who pulled the strings of all the other suspects, including Bruckner.

Alpha.

Castle was the lair of the beast. It was the place from which the criminal mastermind spun his web of deception, death and intrigue. And somewhere in the clandestine super data base maintained by the NSC, Quinn was betting there was a reference to Castle.

"We're in," Quinn said to Ramsey as the computer screen suddenly flashed the message that connection to the data base was initiated.

"But it's asking for an entry code before we can access any information."

"I know," Quinn told her. "Let's try a couple." At the prompt, Quinn input TAURUS.

UNAUTHORIZED ENTRY CODE, the screen flashed.

Quinn swore softly and drummed his fingers on the table. He tried dozens of other words and word combinations, but in every case access was denied. Then, in a flash, he thought of the one word he hadn't tried yet, and suddenly a surge of intuition told him it could be the one he needed.

TRIPSTONE, he typed in at the prompt.

THANK YOU, the screen flashed. STAND BY FOR PROCESSING.

"We're home free," Quinn said to Ramsey. Displayed on the screen were row after row of indexed entry listings. Quinn switched on his printer and began to check off those listings he was interested in accessing.

"How did you know which code would work?" Ramsey asked.

"It was only a guess, really," Quinn replied, his eyes glued to the screen. "Bruckner's code name with Scepter was Tripstone. I figured it was at least worth a shot. Looks like I hit the bull's-eye."

Putting a check mark next to the entry titled CASTLE, Quinn hit the enter key. His printer immediately began to spit out page after page as the columns of data appeared on the screen.

It was all there now, right in front of them. Quinn would have to sift through the hard copy for depth, but what he saw already clarified many mysteries. Castle was a secret no longer, not to Quinn at least.

"Now for the pièce de résistance," Quinn said as he logged off the information to CD storage media and keystroked in another sequence.

"What's that?" Ramsey asked, bending to watch the lines of computer code appearing on the screen.

"A little viral nasty of my own I've cooked up," Quinn returned with a smile. "We don't want to alert anyone to the fact that we've been strolling through their data base at will. This little honey of a Trojan Horse program will neatly cover our tracks but in another ten days will make Bruckner's computer explode in his face the moment he turns it on."

With that, Quinn hit the enter key, loading the electronic booby trap into mass storage memory.

IT WAS THE FALSE DAWN that preceded sunrise, the time when the faintest tinge of cobalt edged the seamless black of night. Out in the coolness of the Nevada desert, away from the lights of any major city, the stars still shone as bright as diamond chips through the clear night air.

Quinn sat behind the wheel of the rental car they had driven from the small local airport outside Reno. He and Ramsey had landed at midnight in the rented plane. They had been driving since then toward their destination.

"There it is," Ramsey said, gesturing ahead of them.

Quinn nodded. He could see it, too.

Looming ahead was the high double row of cyclone fencing beyond which the squat bulks of concrete blockhouses and Quonset huts hunched beneath the gleam of helium-arc perimeter lighting. Although Quinn couldn't see them, he also knew that guards in crow's nests spaced at compass points on high towers thirty feet above the desert floor would soon have the car in the IR sights of their automatic weapons and MANPADS missile launchers. There was no question that the car would have been challenged by now had Quinn and Ramsey not been expected to arrive.

For that matter, had Quinn's covert penetration of the NSC data base network been detected, the vehicle would have been already challenged or blown off the road. The fact that they had gotten this far was partial confirmation that they hadn't been found out yet and fed the hope that they wouldn't be until after their objective was secured.

The penetration of the NSC computer system had been only a prelude to Quinn's next actions. Once he'd made it inside the system, once he had learned the truth concerning Castle, there was another covert computer penetration to be carried out.

It was one that would allow Quinn and Ramsey to penetrate Castle itself. It was the only way in the universe that they could carry out the penetration and destruction of their objective. Though deceptively simple now that Quinn was armed with the classified data he'd acquired via his break-in, it was nevertheless a dangerous gambit.

Bruckner's access code provided the bearer with unrestricted privileges regarding entry to Castle. Once the code was in his possession, Quinn used it as a key to unlock the door to the covert hard-base.

The situation wasn't without irony, Quinn realized. The ancient Greeks had used a gigantic horse fashioned of wood, so legend had it, to sneak their troops past the gates of the citadel of Troy. This act had led to the computer-age slang of "Trojan" when referring to a covert destructive computer code. Now Quinn had broken into a computer network so that he and Ramsey could become human Trojan horses and invade the secret installation.

Suddenly they heard the *thuk-a-thuk* of helicopter rotors churning overhead. The incandescent white light in the sky above was blinding in its intensity. Glancing up through the windshield, Quinn saw the chopper hovering above them, shining the searchlight beacon down on the roof of the car.

"Proceed directly to the main gate," the amplified voice boomed down at them as the pilot's throat mike picked up the vibrations of his larynx. "Follow the instructions of the sentry."

The chopper shadowed the car for the remaining distance until they reached the perimeter of the installation. Then it banked and shot away into the night, its search beacon now damped.

Quinn slid the vehicle up to the main gate of the installation and slowed to take the concrete speed bumps before he stopped short at the striped barrier post. A concrete guardhouse stood to one side.

While the car's engine idled, a soldier in paramilitary camou fatigues stepped from the guardhouse and approached the vehicle. "Your personal identification code word, sir," the guard asked, eyeing Quinn and Ramsey with careful, professional scrutiny.

"Rainbird Sysgen Vail," Quinn said to the guard, speaking clearly.

The guard nodded and produced a small electronic instrument shaped something like a utility flashlight. A small green status light glowed on the side of the device as he held it level with Quinn's face and squeezed the trigger on its pistol-like handgrip.

First Quinn, then Ramsey, stared into the glowing red light of the scanning laser beam. Like the scanner at a supermarket checkout counter, the scanning laser was wrapping itself over every contour of their faces.

It took only a microinstant for its computer chip to compare their faces with the holographic images stored in its data bank. The scanner then emitted two confirmation tones.

The soldier put away the scanner and next produced a one-foot-square touch pad contoured for the human hand. Quinn placed his right hand into the depression on the face of the device.

"Please repeat your code sequence, sir," the soldier instructed him, "and stare into the red light."

"Rainbird Sysgen Vail," Quinn said, speaking evenly as the microprocessor compared his fingerprints, voice and retinal patterns with those stored in memory.

The touch pad, too, emitted a confirmation tone, whereupon the soldier subjected Ramsey to the same sequence of thorough identity checks.

"Thank you," the soldier told them when the checks were completed. "Proceed directly to departure area number three. It's directly ahead and indicated by arrows."

The soldier added nothing more, nor did he smile. The people who passed routinely through the gates of the installation weren't the kind one smiled at. They weren't the kind who were used to being smiled at, either. They had numbers instead of names and ice water in their veins.

They were also individuals who generally carried no identification. It was the single most glaring flaw in the Castle security control system that

Quinn was counting on to enable himself and Ramsey to enter the clandestine hardbase.

The godlike technology that the spooks routinely used made them slaves to its ability to screen the truth from falsehood, reality from unreality. The battery of ID checks were considered virtually flawless, capable of detecting all unauthorized entrants, who would then be executed without trial on capture.

But the opposition's own fetish for secrecy had given Quinn the back door he needed to enter Castle. The voice prints, facial holograms, palm prints and other identification data had all been Quinn's creations, manufactured at the computer terminal.

The data belonged to Quinn and Ramsey but were now linked to fictitious names and professional histories that Quinn had covertly inserted into the computer data banks. These digitized "legends" now went with the faces and other identifying data that he had also scanned into the system.

Until such time as the penetration and data tampering were detected, Quinn and Ramsey would be known by the code names Berber and Fleet, deep-cover operatives so secret that not even the ultrasophisticated NSA computer at Fort Meade knew anything of their whereabouts.

Operatives of an organization that Quinn had thought long ago disbanded, an organization he had resigned from when he discovered the depths of its corruption, an organization that still carried out its lethal business under a different guise.

Scepter.

25

"Is that the—?" Ramsey began to ask.

"Yeah. That's it," Quinn replied, tight-lipped.

He, too, had simultaneously observed the black, smoothly contoured structure that was silhouetted against the lightening horizon. Adrenaline coursed through his system at the thought of the chain reaction of events that would come next.

Moments later they reached the second security checkpoint where an armed guard halted the car and asked for the gate passes they had been handed by the first sentry. Quinn and Ramsey presented the guard with their gate passes, which bore their holographic likenesses imprinted on each Mylar card. He compared both of these, then handed back the passes.

"Park in one of the free bays," he instructed Quinn. "Then climb aboard."

The soldier indicated the APC—armored personnel carrier—that waited a few score feet away, engine idling. He watched Quinn and Ramsey through gimlet eyes as they exited their vehicle and walked the short distance to the APC.

The personnel carrier's unspeaking driver immediately got the vehicle mobile and began rolling across the wide apron of tarmac toward the black object that Quinn and Ramsey had seen on their arrival at the high-security area a few minutes before.

It was an ASP or aerospace plane, a hypersonic scramjet with runway-to-orbit capability, one of the few such advanced aircraft that had been constructed since the end of the space shuttle era in the mid-nineties.

Bearing no identifying markings, the aircraft's profile displayed the rounded curvatures characteristic of stealthy aerodynamic surfaces. Its nose assembly was disklike and flattened, and its mission-adaptable wings canted slightly forward from the sides of the fuselage. Engine nacelles were incorporated into the framework of the wings, and the engines themselves were sunk deep into the airframe. The plane resembled an immense mechanical manta ray.

The scramjet was the key to penetrating the place known as Castle.

Quinn and Ramsey were again asked to present their gate passes to the armed guard posted by the scramjet. Then they entered the plane via the boarding ramp. The interior of the aircraft was outfitted with seating for twenty-five passengers.

Ramsey and Quinn strapped themselves into their seats. The pilot was already warming up the high-pressure propane-oxygen thrusters as the hatch shut with a muted hiss of hydraulic pressure. Now the two agents were sealed within the fuselage of the advanced hypersonic aircraft.

"Estimated flight time twenty-two minutes," the voice of the pilot said, coming in over the cockpit-to-cabin intercom link. "Please remain seated until you receive permission to debark."

Soon the manta-shaped, black-hulled paramilitary aircraft began taxiing onto the runway. The takeoff of the space plane was like that of any conventional supersonic jet. In fact, the supersonic combustion ramjet or "scramjet" turbines that powered the space plane in hypersonic flight would function as ordinary jet engines while the aircraft remained in the lower atmosphere.

Quinn felt himself pressed back into his seat as the cabin tilted sharply upward. They gained altitude quickly and were soon many thousands of feet off the ground.

Unlike a conventional jet aircraft, however, the space-capable sky streaker didn't level off at thirty thousand feet. Instead it continued to climb straight up until the sky, which had already turned a deep indigo with the passing of night, again turned pitch-black. Finally the aircraft reached its hypersonic cruising speed of Mach 25 at an altitude of nearly eighty thousand feet.

Quinn knew that they were at the edge of space. Outside the cabin window he could again see the stars, but they were far brighter now, blazing through the microatmosphere at that altitude like hot sparks. Below him, through light cloud cover, a thin sliver of a brilliant blue earth was also visible.

Inside the cockpit the computer generated eyes-up display of the pilot's advanced avionics system flashed graphical data indicating that the fly-by-wire navigational system had locked onto the docking coordinates preprogrammed into its onboard flight computer system.

Beams of invisible microwave laser radiation were lancing through the microatmosphere, obtaining a flight profile confirmation on the orbiting entity that was the space plane's destination.

Quinn looked out the cabin window and thought he saw their destination somewhere in the distance, visible against the blackness of near space, but he couldn't be certain. Castle had, after all, been designed and constructed to be virtually invisible from ground- or space-based detection systems.

America's experiments with Star Wars technology had been funded by billions of dollars since its inception in the last years of the Reagan and early years of the Bush administrations, and perfected during the succeeding administration. Billions more dollars, however, had been secretly funneled into the fund of a covert project, a project intended to insert a stealth-equipped military space station into earth-orbit by the beginning of the twenty-first century.

The code name for this project was Castle.

What had begun as "a castle in the air" in the minds of secret war planners had ultimately become translated into the most ambitious clandestine project in the history of American covert planning. Stealth construction materials and architecture had been integrated into the orbital station's design to make Castle invisible to the probing beams from the ground, air or space.

Its stealthy design would reduce its radar signature so that all ELINT devices would see it as a piece of orbiting space junk. Intelligence and private-sector computers had been covertly programmed with a "legend" identifying the station as an aging telecommunications satellite in a decaying orbit too erratic to permit safe approaches to the sector by spacecraft.

From its orbit in space, Castle also evaded detection by means of sophisticated electronic cloaking. The space platform was shrouded in a latticework of laser beams that had the effect of refracting visible light, making Castle appear optically transparent. Both the human eye and video sensors would merely detect a star field tinged with only a faint translucency to indicate that a solid object might, in fact, be hanging in their field of view.

Of course, they would first have to know precisely where to look. This was because the stealthy station's orbit was constantly changing and its exact coordinates were as secret as the existence of Castle itself.

Somehow the man known as Alpha had gained control of Castle and turned the orbiting platform into his private domain. From Castle he had set about to undermine the world's last shot at energy independence from fossil fuels for reasons that were at the moment best known to Alpha himself.

Quinn didn't yet know the precise nature of the link between Castle and the deaths of the Prometheus technicians, but he was certain a link ex-

isted. Castle was inextricably connected with the
plot to undermine the Prometheus Net and the
bloody chain of global homicides. When Quinn
boarded Castle, he hoped finally to learn the whys
and wherefores of that link and put an end to the
wave of terror that had been sweeping the earth.

Three rapid tones signaled that they were about
to make their final approach to the assigned
docking module. The navigational computers were
already zeroing in on the covert space station's
transponder beacon. Minutes later the space-
capable aircraft was nestled safely in its berth.

Quinn and Ramsey were ordered to remain
seated until the module's inner airlock chamber
was pressurized to an earth level of one atmosphere. When the docking module's pressure became equal to the interior cabin pressure, the
hatch would be opened and the ASP's two passengers would then be allowed to exit.

Quinn and Ramsey deplaned as soon as the atmospheric interlock was sealed and the pressure on
both sides of the module was equalized at one atmosphere. Sentries wearing gray jumpsuits and
armed with advanced-design bullpup weapons
waited inside the module's debarkation ramp.
Quinn and Ramsey were again asked to present the
passes that had been issued at the ASP's earth-

based clandestine launch facility. One of the sentries took the passes from both "Berber" and "Fleet" and passed them through.

It had seemed to go well until they spotted Bruckner was waiting for them at the end of the ramp. By contrast with the armed security squad that stood behind him, all attired in gray jumpsuits, he was wearing a black jumpsuit and high lace-up combat boots. A handgun bulged in the pit holster that he wore crosswise on his barrel chest, and the stubby black cone of a sound-suppressor protruded through the open bottom of the holster.

A broad smile was on his perpetually flushed face as Bruckner slid the pistol from his chest rig and, extending his right arm, pointed its business end at Quinn's chest. "Nice try," he growled, even as the security men ran forward and jammed their weapons into the two agents' backs, "but no cigar, kemo sabe."

Bruckner squeezed the trigger of the weapon clutched in his hand. The gun wheezed twice in quick succession, and Quinn saw the corridor's overhead lights suddenly tilt and streak into space.

Then the darkness engulfed him.

26

Quinn awoke suddenly, jerking upright from a half-remembered nightmare. The room was small, bare, white and antiseptic. His head ached like hell and his chest throbbed painfully where the tranquilizer dart fired by Bruckner had pierced his flesh.

Shaking his head to clear it, Quinn took stock of his situation. As he had expected, the Glock side arm he'd carried in a shoulder holster was missing, as well as his watch, wallet and belt.

It would also have been standard operating procedure for his captors to subject him to a broad-spectrum scan for other concealed weapons before throwing him into the cell.

It was a cell, of course. Quinn had no doubt about it.

Still groggy from the effects of the drug, he went to the door and pressed random sequences on the touch pad on the wall beside it. The door didn't open. Quinn tried forcing it but it wouldn't slide open, either.

Confirmed: it was a cell.

Quinn knew also that Bruckner's goons would come for him soon. They might be watching him now, probably were via concealed pinhead-size fiber-optic video cameras that could be hidden anywhere in the room.

If his captors had him under surveillance, they would know by now that he had come around. So waiting for them was the only option left open to Quinn. He decided he would maximize his tactical position. When they came for him, he would be ready.

Standing atop the low-rise stainless-steel gurney on which they had placed him, Quinn was just able to reach the lighting panel on the drop ceiling. He slid the crackle-finished plastic square from its slot in the support framework and reached inside the crawl space to unplug the lighting tube from its electrical socket.

The room was immediately plunged into total darkness. Quinn knew that if anyone was watching him, they wouldn't expect a captive to act in the manner he had acted. They would be disoriented. If their psych-out game called for disorienting the captive, then Quinn would have suddenly changed the ground rules.

Quinn rolled the stainless-steel gurney to one side of the door on its trundle wheels. He didn't think the fiber-optic video was low-light or passive IR. There was no need for it here, and the additional technology would demand a trade-off in sensor size. Since there was no overt sign of surveillance cameras, Quinn felt he could assume that the pinpoint lenses sure to be present incorporated no low-light observation features.

Quinn lowered himself into a comfortable sitting position beside the stainless-steel table and waited, engaging in hwa rang do breathing exercises to clear his mind of the lingering aftereffects of the knockout drug.

At first the darkness was total, the silence complete, broken only by the faintest hairline of light seeping in from the corridor outside the cell and the faint sounds of Castle's life-support system from deep within the station. Soon, though, Quinn's eyes and ears adjusted to the new visual environment to the point where he could make out the blurred outlines of the table in front of him and the lock pad beside the door.

A moment later Quinn heard the sound of footfalls from the corridor outside. He knew that the moment of reckoning was coming.

He had spooked them. Now he had to be ready for what would happen next.

The cell door slid open, its electronic lock activated by the correct combination entered from the outside. Framed in the doorway, a guard's silhouette loomed suddenly in the light streaming in from the corridor.

The jumpsuited trooper hesitated for a moment, his SMG ported at the ready as he peered into the darkness of the cell. Then, cautiously, he ventured a step inside.

Quinn shoved hard against the heavy steel cart and sent it hurtling toward the guard. It struck the man squarely in the shins, hurling him off balance. Quinn was on him instantly, taking advantage of the guard's surprise to press home his attack.

Following through on his shutout play, Quinn lashed out with a fist to the guard's jaw that splintered teeth and fractured bone. With a grunt of pain the guard suddenly let go of his SMG. It spun from his nerveless fingers, striking the floor of the cell with a crash.

Quinn whirled from the injured guard and made a fast grab for the weapon lying on the floor. A sideways swipe and the guard was down for the count.

Fists now bulging with steel-blue heat, Nomad was loose in the corridor a second later, blinking against the sudden intensity of the light from the overhead lighting panels in the corridor ceiling. Turning abruptly, though, he saw that he wasn't alone in the corridor. Bruckner and a squad of Castle guards were waiting a little farther along, weapons pointing menacingly at him.

Quinn did a half turn to the other side and saw more guards deployed at the other end of the corridor. The passageway was sealed off and Quinn was boxed in.

"You're smooth, kemo sabe," Bruckner said to him with a smile. "But I'm king of the hill. Now drop the weapon and kick it away from you. You don't have any cards left to play."

Quinn wasn't holding squat, and he knew he had nothing to bluff with. He placed the commandeered SMG on the corridor deck and kicked it to one side as Bruckner instructed him.

"That's smart," Bruckner acknowledged, nodding. "Put your hands up and clasp them behind your head."

There was a sudden movement behind Quinn as he complied. Out of the corner of his eye Quinn saw the Castle guard he'd wounded in the fight stagger from the cell he'd just escaped from. Blood was trickling from the corners of the

guard's mouth, staining his gray jun.
brown.

"Look what you did to him," Bruckne.
Quinn, shaking his head morosely. "I'm
I'm going to have to make an example out of you,
babycakes."

Bruckner ordered the injured man to step to one
side and raised the silenced automatic pistol in his
hands to aim its stubby muzzle at Quinn's face.

Quinn braced for the bullet that would claim his
life as he stared unflinchingly into Bruckner's
homicidal blue eyes. Just before Bruckner's finger passed the breakpoint, though, he suddenly
jerked the weapon to one side.

The sound-suppressed automatic pistol coughed
once, and the head of the injured guard who stood
to one side of Quinn broke apart into bloody jig-
saw puzzle pieces. Spun half around by the force
of the bullet, the guard crashed into the bulkhead
and slid down to the deck in a sitting position,
leaving a bloody trail behind him.

Bruckner tucked the silenced blaster into the pit
holster he wore riding high on his barrel chest.
"You can put your hands down now, kemo sabe,"
he said to Quinn with a demented grin.

AFTER HE was force-marched along the corridor at
gunpoint, Quinn rode a high-capacity utility ele-

vator down a few levels. When the doors opened, he found himself in a large round-walled operations bay with a ceiling that rose at least thirty feet.

"Come with me," Bruckner ordered him.

Quinn was led toward an isolated bank of instrument consoles raised from the others in the bay on a glass-encased observation platform. Another gray-uniformed man was seated at the workstation in a chair before the bank of constantly phasing view screens.

He spun around as Bruckner approached.

The man had no face.

To the naked eye it appeared to be a puttylike gray mask with only the vaguest traces of eyes, nose, ears and mouth to indicate the human visage. Quinn knew this was the result of sophisticated electronic masking that refracted light in such a way as to distort the image his eyes received.

Quinn was aware he was in the presence of the supercriminal they called Alpha.

"Mr. Quinn," Alpha said to the newcomer. His voice, too—a cold, metallic-sounding whisper—was an electronic simulation. It went with the optically distorted face. "How good of you to honor us with your presence." Alpha stood. He was tall, almost as tall as Quinn himself. "Leave us," he said to Bruckner.

"Where's Ramsey?" Quinn growled at Alpha as Bruckner went away.

"She is alive," Alpha's inhuman mechanical voice returned after a brief pause. "Perhaps you would care to see her?"

Without waiting for a reply, Alpha turned and keystroked in a command set at the keyboard of the workstation at which he stood. A large, flat digital screen flickered immediately to life.

Quinn was looking down at Ramsey, who sat with her head slumped limply between her shoulders. For a moment she looked up at the hidden video sensor head and made a forlorn moaning sound. Quinn could see the dark purple marks of bruises on her face.

"She was a reluctant participant in some amusing games," Alpha said in his eerily soft voice, "but don't worry. She is safe, at least for the present. As for you, we would like you to see what we have accomplished here while we decided whether to dispose of you or not."

The words came out evenly, emotionlessly, as though life and death were inconsequential trifles. With Bruckner following close behind, Castle's mastermind turned on his heels and walked toward a nearby access elevator.

As Alpha led Quinn below through the command-and-control center of the covert space station, Quinn found that he was indeed impressed. Giant view screens provided instant real-time telemetry of all earth- and space-based targets. At banks of data terminals operatives in gray coveralls were busily at work. Beyond the command center Alpha stopped before the large windows of an observation area.

"You rightly supposed that the deaths of the Prometheus technicians were connected to Castle," Alpha told Quinn as they stood looking out one of the picture windows at the earth below. "They knew the details of this installation, and so had to die."

"The first suicides, how were they accomplished?" Quinn asked.

"Our most capable operative Taurus saw to those easily enough," Alpha's electronic voice replied. "It was an easy enough matter to implant a microminiature device in the skull of each. The implant resulted in suicidal actions. The remaining technicians could not be so easily implanted for various reasons, including limited time."

"And that's where I fitted into the picture," Quinn said, "to set them up so your hitters could knock them down."

"Precisely, Mr. Quinn," Alpha answered, then turned back toward the viewing window. "From this vantage point the world looks so pristine, so pure, so unified. Don't you think so, Mr. Quinn?" he asked after a beat.

"Yes," Quinn returned. "But so what?" Quinn knew he had to keep Alpha talking. Once an adversary began talking, his control began to erode. While the opposition talked it was time to think, think desperately about a way out of the trap Alpha had prepared.

"But it is anything but pristine," Alpha went on calmly. "Chaos rules below. Mankind infests the planet with a plague of violence. We will put an end to the violence. We will usher in a new era of universal peace and cooperation."

"How?" Quinn asked. "Just how do you propose to do that?"

"By using Prometheus, of course," Alpha responded. "The Prometheus satellite network is the key to our grand design. The satellites can radiate clean, safe energy to power the machinery mankind depends on."

Alpha threw back his head and stretched out his arms as if to embrace the entire shining blue planet as it hung in space below the orbital station.

"Of course, the tremendous energy they radiate can also rip a gaping hole in the ozone layer capable of obliterating all life on earth. It was we who placed the virus within the computer system," he continued. "From Castle we now control it."

"And you want tribute," Quinn stated.

"No, not merely tribute. We wish to fulfill our birthright. If the nations of the world agree to our just demands for unified control of all world governments, then Prometheus will be allowed to fulfill its mission. If not, then we'll unleash death and terror on a scale never before seen."

"You're out of your mind," Quinn said flatly.

Alpha paused. "We had hoped you might not feel that way, Mr. Quinn," his mechanical voice said with perfect calm. "We had even hoped you might be persuaded to join us, as Taurus has done. That is why we did not kill you originally as Taurus insisted we do. Now we see that he was right all along."

Alpha signaled to Bruckner, who was waiting on the sidelines. At a nod from the rogue spook, security men rushed forward and grabbed hold of

Quinn's arms. Drawing his silenced piece, Bruckner motioned with it for them to hold Quinn prisoner.

"What do you want me to do with him?" Bruckner asked his faceless, emotionless master.

"Kill him, of course," Alpha told his enforcer, then turned back to contemplate the beauty of the glowing blue planet hanging in the darkness of space below him.

27

"Wish I could say I was sorry, Quinn," Bruckner told him as Quinn was marched at gunpoint to one of the space station's airlock modules. "But since I'm gonna enjoy doing you to the max, I guess I won't bother pretending."

"You're all heart, Bruckner," Quinn told him.

"And you're history, kemo sabe," Bruckner countered as they reached the place he had decided would be perfect for punching his former protégé's ticket.

The airlock permitted access to the space station's exterior. Repair crews used it to conduct routine maintenance to the outer hull, which was regularly bombarded by thousands of meteoroid strikes per day.

Bruckner motioned to one of the members of the Castle security crew flanking them to open the inner airlock hatch with a keystroked command on the touch pad beside the electronic doorway. The heavy armored panel slid into the bulkhead with a soft whir, revealing the airlock chamber. At its far end was a second sliding hatchway that closed off the black void of outer space. For Quinn the outer hatch was the last stop before a free-fall through an eternal vacuum.

"What we're gonna do here, Quinn," Bruckner went on once the inner hatch was fully opened, "is turn you into one more piece of orbiting space junk."

The security crew guffawed loudly at this remark, but Bruckner silenced them with a wave of his hand.

"Of course you'll eventually burn up in the atmosphere like any piece of space debris once your orbit decays," he went on, "but we all burn out sooner or later, don't we, *compadre?*"

Without pausing a beat, Bruckner lashed out against the side of Quinn's jaw with the side of the heavy steel barrel of the silenced automatic in his hand. The vicious, unexpected blow sent Quinn reeling into the airlock, whereupon Bruckner immediately shut the hatch again.

"That's much better." Bruckner said once the hatch was made completely airtight, speaking into a commo grille set into the door frame.

On the other side of the airlock hatch Quinn heard Bruckner's voice rasping over the opposite speaker grille.

"Now, as I was saying, kemo sabe, we're gonna see exactly what you're made of. I mean that in more ways than one, since once the air pressure drops to zero your internal pressure should make you pop right open."

More guffawing from the contingent of sky troopers accompanied Bruckner's last remark.

Quinn picked himself up off the deck plates and mentally tuned Bruckner out. He knew there was more than garden-variety sadism in Bruckner's taunts. The man was trying to psych him out, neutralize his capability to think of a way out before he pulled the chain on him. But Quinn knew that the most important thing now was to concentrate on his predicament, find a means of evading the terrible death that was intended for him.

There was an LED readout panel above the outer hatchway that was counting down toward zero. Quinn didn't need Bruckner's macabre play-by-play to grasp the fact that when zero came up the outer hatch would slide open and Quinn would be sucked out into the icy cold and total vacuum of space.

Working quickly, Quinn removed his shirt and feverishly started tearing it into strips roughly an inch in width. The opposition had checked him over for weapons and had stripped him of his gun. Quinn had anticipated they would.

Since there had been a strong possibility that his gambit to enter Castle would be discovered before his arrival, he knew that any weapon he carried would be forfeit. However, since he would also certainly be searched and stripped of any weapon, he needed something special. So he had masked his true weapon by taking along a side arm and spare ammo clips.

Quinn had counted on whoever searched him to miss the real weapons he was carrying concealed on his person, and they apparently had done just that. Quinn's shirt was woven of a special polymer, an insensitive munitions compound that was inert except when detonated by a precisely determined method. To do that he had to use a special chemical detonator. It then became a high-energy explosive.

Detonation was based on the time pencil principle first used by the OSS in the Second World War. The time pencil detonators used chemical as opposed to mechanical detonators to set off munitions charges.

Quinn's chemical time pencil was actually more like a time splinter. The tiny snippets of wirelike plastic alloy were each coded by color for detonation duration. Quinn had secreted them in the stiffener of his shirt collar.

Now he selected the red time splinter, preset to detonate in ten seconds, and inserted it into one end of the strip of shirt fabric, which he had twisted into a tight strand and laid across the bolted-down square on the floor. It was Quinn's hope that the square covered a service node for the station's fiber-optic conduits.

Arming the time splinter by bending it double, Quinn stepped back against the airlock bulkhead. Right on cue ten seconds later the high-energy explosive detonated with a muffled report.

The low-decibel but high-yield blast punched a hole in the steel plate. The hole looked barely wide enough for a man to slither through on hands and knees. Squatting, Quinn tried to squeeze his body into the rupture in the deck.

To his dismay he found that it was too narrow. He took a deep breath and forced himself to relax, expelling all the air in his lungs and contracting his stomach and chest muscles.

On his next attempt to squeeze into the hole, Quinn succeeded in wedging his body through the aperture in the deck and hoped that there was crawl space below him. As it turned out, there was.

The crawl space extended downward to a depth of about ten feet. It then branched sideways to dovetail with the main line of a maintenance shaft infrastructure that connected every section of the orbiting space platform.

Inching his way along the narrow tunnel on all fours, Quinn struggled to put as much distance as he could between himself and the airlock above him. He was only too well aware that he had mere seconds to spare before the lock timer caused the outer airlock hatch to open.

Once that happened the powerful vacuum of space would begin sucking atmosphere up through the conduit. If Quinn was too close to the airlock when it decompressed, the force of the violent suction might conceivably be great enough to pull his body back through the shaft, either ejecting him into space or trapping him where he would slowly asphyxiate in the remaining microthin air.

Suddenly a tremendous whoosh of air was sucked up into the tunnel behind him. Quinn felt the tug of the powerful suction at his back and heard the roar of atmosphere being drawn up through the hole in the ruptured floor plate at high speed.

Now he knew that the airlock hatch had opened above him and that the lock was rapidly decompressing. Fighting the powerful wind drag, Quinn crawled forward on elbows and knees as fast as he was able.

"That's enough," Bruckner said to his men after a few minutes had elapsed. "Open the hatch."

The man on his right punched in the code that opened the airlock, and the hatchway slid back into the bulkhead after the chamber was repressurized. Bruckner stepped inside the resealed airlock and stood there with his lantern jaw agape. He had immediately spotted the hole that Quinn had blown in the floor plate.

"He's gone!" he shouted. "Damn it. Order a condition-one alert! Find him. And when you do, dust the bastard on sight!"

28

Klaxons shrieked in Quinn's ears as he peered into the corridor beyond a rectangular wire-mesh grille. The grille wasn't securely bolted to the duct cowling that held it in place. Striking out with the heels of his hands, he was able to dislodge the grille from its cowling, and he pulled it sideways into the duct behind him as noiselessly as possible.

Pausing before exiting the vent, he listened and watched for any indications of activity coming from the corridor beyond. He detected none.

Quinn quickly eased himself down from the rectangular space in the bulkhead of the space station. The muscles of his thighs cushioned the impact of landing, silencing his entry into the corridor.

Nomad moved like a cat on the balls of his feet, hugging the wall. With the Klaxons blaring he didn't hear the sound of the door opening to his right and just stepped back in time to avoid crashing headlong into a technician who seemed to be in a great hurry.

The tech was carrying a clipboard in his hand and said a few hasty words over his shoulder to someone inside the room as he raced out into the corridor and disappeared around a bend. Quinn heard the sound of nearby elevator doors trundling open and then closing again.

He strained his ears but detected no other presence nearby. He rapped on the door from which the tech had emerged. As soon as it was open a crack, he forced himself inside.

Though taken by surprise, the lone Castle technician managed to pull a knife, but he never got the chance to use it. Quinn slammed him against the wall and applied pressure to his windpipe. The knife fell from suddenly inert fingers.

The face of the man in the white jumpsuit twisted up in a mixture of surprise and terror. With desperate strength he broke free and made an attempt to reach the door leading to the corridor.

Quinn smashed him across the face with a hard right that fractured his cheekbone. Then he hauled the bleeding tech to his feet and pushed him up against the wall again with his elbow across the man's trachea. He applied steady pressure until he heard cartilage snap and the tech slid down the side of the wall, unconscious.

Moving fast, Quinn stripped the man, then deposited him and the bundle of his own clothes behind a lab table. Now dressed as a tech, minus the downed man's glasses, Quinn stepped into the corridor. The Klaxons that signaled a condition-one alert status were still wailing nonstop as he rounded a dogleg in the corridor.

A squad of Castle guardsmen were heading straight toward him, moving at a fast trot, weapons at the ready. Quinn buttonholed the commander who was bringing up the rear of the squad.

"Just a minute," he said to the guy, feigning timidity. "I caught a fellow in my lab who had no business being there. Fortunately I was able to knock him senseless using a beam scale before he noticed I was behind him."

The soldier regarded the tech through narrowed eyes. "You sure about that?" he asked gruffly.

"Oh, I'm quite positive," Quinn replied. He was already leading the way for the obliging guardsman. "Here it is. Right inside. He's unconscious, but I think you'd better be careful. He looked quite dangerous."

"Don't worry about me, computer weenie," the soldier barked as he stepped inside and pointed his

SMG at the moaning figure lying behind a lab table.

Stepping quickly behind the soldier, Quinn hit him over the head with a stainless-steel centrifuge he had snatched from a lab table. But he controlled the blow so that it wouldn't smash into the man's head full force. The guard crumpled to the deck, temporarily unconscious.

Quinn brought the hardguy around by dumping a beaker full of distilled water into his face. He had a couple of questions to ask the trooper before he was through with him.

"You know who I am," Quinn told the groggy man, shoving the point of his own commandeered SMG into his face.

"Yeah, I know you are," he grunted in pain and anger.

"The woman who came with me," Quinn went on, prodding the man with the muzzle of the SMG, "I want to know where she is."

"I don't know," the sky soldier groaned.

"That's the wrong answer. Next time I'm going to start shooting, starting with your knees and moving up. Don't say I didn't warn you."

A quick glance at Quinn's hard face convinced the man that he meant business. "Node Five, D-

Section. One of the holding cells there. It's no big secret, anyway."

"You better be right, or I'll come back and take you apart."

"I swear it, pal. I'm telling you the truth."

Believing the frightened trooper, Quinn gagged and stripped him, then tied his hands behind him using a length of wire from the lab's equipment. Then Quinn exchanged the guard's gray paramilitary jumpsuit for the all-white lab clothes. The reassuring feel of the SMG in his fists and the minigrenades hanging from ALICE webbing felt extra good.

Quinn took one more look inside the lab, satisfying himself that everything was in order, then let himself out. In the corridor he used the Spectre's heavy buttplate to smash the combination touch pad to useless scrap. It would hopefully put the electronically activated door out of commission in the event the other technician decided to return to the lab.

Pandemonium held sway throughout the corridors of the covert space station. Gray-clad Castle guardsmen were mobilizing everywhere, searching frantically for the intruder in their midst.

Quinn might have been the single solitary human being on board Castle at that moment who

had any clear conception of where he was going
and what he was doing.

He had two objectives. The first concerned
dealing a terminal blow to Castle's operational
capabilities.

The multibillion-dollar piece of high-tech space
hardware was nothing more than another covert
military boondoggle in his eyes. It had been designed and constructed at the behest of men with
a ruthless, unquenchable thirst for power.

Quinn had originally set out to destroy this orbiting headquarters. Nomad's objective was now
to destroy the criminal mastermind called Alpha
along with his stealth-cloaked eyrie in the heavens.

Quinn had pored over computer schematics of
the space platform when he hacked his way into
the clandestine data base prior to forging the electronic passes he'd used to get himself and Ramsey
aboard the ASP. He was aware that the station's
weakest point was the nuclear reactor that powered all on-board systems, including life-support
infrastructure, hydroponic machinery, gravity
synthesizers and the solid-fuel rocket thrusters that
moved its ever-changing orbital trajectories.

Destroying the nuclear reactor that pumped the
energy lifeblood through Castle meant effectively

ripping out its heart. That was what Quinn aimed
to do as he quickly made his way toward the in-
nermost level of Castle. Area maps posted on the
walls gave clear directions to all sections of the
orbiting sky base.

Dressed in the commandeered paramilitary
outfit he'd taken from the downed trooper, and in
the confusion that held sway everywhere in Castle, Quinn went unrecognized as he took the elevator down to the central power plant at the core
node of the space station. Two guards were posted
at a checkpoint directly ahead as he stepped from
the elevator car into the corridor surrounding a
vast chamber he could see through windows behind them. The chamber housed banks of flashing instrument panels and clusters of humming
machinery.

The guards regarded him suspiciously as he approached.

"You two," Quinn said peremptorily. "You're
both wanted up at comm center on the double.
Didn't you hear the page?"

They almost started to move on, but something
made them turn back to him. "Hey, wait a minute," one of them said as his eyes went to the name
tag on Quinn's right chest, noticing that the name

and face didn't match. "You're not Henderson. You're—"

But he never got the chance to say another word. Quinn had already whipped the SMG to assault position and had unleashed a blistering PB fire that blew the soldier off his feet.

The man's partner managed to get off a quick, stuttering burst from his SMG, but Quinn cut him down, too, and the 9 mm salvo did no more than pock the bulkhead with bullet holes. Above the maddening screech of the alert Klaxons Quinn hoped the sound of autofire wouldn't carry far.

Quinn fished the key to the generator node hatch from the pockets of one of the dead men, then slid the credit-card-sized key into the slot to one side of the lock touch pad and the hatch slid open. There were a couple more guards stationed on a catwalk on the other side, and Quinn took out both with two quick bursts.

He was now alone on the catwalk that surrounded the mammoth generator room where the turbine wail of powerful machinery rose to a whining crescendo. Metal ladders zigzagged up to the steel catwalk from which technicians could monitor the status of the furiously revving electrical conversion equipment.

At the center of the huge pit stood the nuclear engine that converted sunlight into electrical power with the aid of solar collection panels. The nuclear dynamo was slated to be Quinn's next target. Destroy this structure, and he could send the entire station raining down to terra firma in small glowing chunks of orbital debris. Quinn hurried down into the pit at the foot of the catwalk.

He didn't see the tech rise quietly from one of the banks of computer workstations and swing the heavy wrench at his head. Quinn heard the whistle of the bludgeon slicing the air, though, and spun around just in time to avoid getting the side of his skull caved in.

The blow went completely wide of its intended mark, and Quinn put his opponent out of the running with a double-fisted, full-bodied swipe of the SMG's buttstock.

Quinn then proceeded to check out one of the control panels. The menu-driven, knowledge-based software that governed the operation of the power station apparatus looked easy to penetrate and master.

In no time flat Quinn hacked his way into the central processor module's software user interface. This meant he now effectively had his hand on the throttle of the base's nuclear turbine.

A quick check of the software command menu provided Quinn with several different slants on how he might rig the nuclear reactor to program itself to reach critical mass fast. Total, irreversible destruction would then be only a keystroke or two away.

Just then Quinn abruptly heard a weird clanking sound behind him and to his left. Coiled-spring reflexes whirled him around just in time to see a familiar yet at the same time bizarre figure approaching from the elevator bank.

It was Bruckner.

What was unfamiliar about Bruckner was the metallic superstructure that now cocooned his barrel-chested torso, head, legs and arms. It was a cocoon of gleaming stainless steel, and it made the man look invincible.

"Jig's up, kemo sabe!" Bruckner shouted. "Ditch the shooter. With this ultrahard titanium-stainless-steel alloy body armor I'm wearing, those nines might as well be peas from a soda straw."

Although Quinn fired off a Spectre salvo without hesitation, it turned out that Bruckner was telling the truth. The ricocheting steel-jacketed Parabellum rounds merely spanged off the combat cocoon without leaving behind so much as a dent.

Reaching down suddenly, Bruckner peeled off a hunk of floor plating as though it were a sheet of aluminum foil, despite its rows of mounting rivet heads. Taurus hurled the sixty-pound hunk of ragged-edged steel plate like a discus. Sidestepping quickly, Quinn heard the earsplitting crash as the lethal debris crashed into the console at which he'd been seated. Circuits flew with loud popping sounds as hot yellow sparks cascaded to the deck. The ionized air filled with the noxious stench of ozone.

"Just a little demonstration to show you what this advanced body-armor cocoon is capable of, good buddy," Bruckner said with a demented laugh. "Now it's time to face the music and dance."

Bruckner began lumbering forward on servomotorized metal legs. Quinn raised the SMG and fired off another salvo, but the slugs merely bounced off the high-tensile-strength stainless-steel exoskeleton like so many dried beans. Reaching out, Bruckner cackled dementedly and snatched the automatic weapon from Quinn's fists.

Then, with his mechanically augmented fist, he crushed the SMG's drop-forged steel receiver as though it were a beer can and flung the now useless heap of scrap metal clear across the huge chamber.

"You poor dumb S.O.B.," Bruckner growled as he charged Quinn. "You just pissed me off bigtime."

29

Quinn hurled himself to one side across a long instrumentation panel studded with flashing buttons, digital readout displays and video terminals as the killing machine bore down on him. Bruckner's momentum propelled him forward, and his stainless-steel-sheathed fist came hammering down onto the panel with tremendous force. Instead of striking Quinn, the fist crashed like a mace into the metal surface of the instrument panel, sending sparks cascading and billows of acrid smoke geysering into the air.

The pneumatic servos powering Bruckner's combat cocoon whined and grated as they labored to free the fist trapped in the twisted metal wreckage. Straightening up now that he'd gotten loose, Bruckner spun around to face his antagonist.

He turned left and right, but Quinn was nowhere to be seen. "You can run, kemo sabe, but you can't hide," the rogue spook shouted as he strode lengthwise through the rows of instrument panels like a vengeful Titan. "Dying's about the only option you've got left."

Just ahead of Bruckner, Quinn crouched between two other banks of control panels. Two mini-grenades were clutched in his fists. As he came abreast of the next bank of instrument panels, Bruckner saw Quinn jump from cover and hurl the two small black globes at him.

Bruckner got out of harm's way with surprising speed for a man wearing a half-ton armored exoskeleton, but the bouncing submunitions detonated close enough to catch him in the lethal radius of their blast and splinter zone. The traitorous agent hit the deck with a thunderous crash that resounded through the huge chamber. Caustic smoke rushed up from the hardsuit's overloaded power servos and from damaged instrumentation clusters on the panels nearby.

Quinn cautiously approached the still-immobile spook in the hardened combat rig. Suddenly he saw Bruckner shudder like a man fitfully returning to consciousness. Sweeping his arms beneath him, Bruckner slowly and laboriously climbed to his feet.

The concussion and shrapnel from the grenades had done only minor damage to Bruckner's combat armor. Blast effect had flung him to the deck, and his ears rang like fire alarms, but the suit's fail-soft systems reported sustainable damage.

The upshot was that Bruckner was still ready to rock and roll.

"No show, Quinn!" he shouted. "You didn't do anything except piss me off. Now it's my turn to beat on you, old buddy."

Bruckner advanced on Quinn with rapid strides on servomechanized legs. Quinn dodged nimbly out of his heavier, slower adversary's grasp, sheltering behind a row of squat, cylindrical chemical-waste canisters.

As Bruckner came nearer, Quinn opened the valves and spigots protruding from piping that ran between the tanks, releasing a flood of oily, green-black waste liquid that gushed from the canisters in a furious stream.

The steel boot soles of Bruckner's combat exoskeleton had trouble negotiating through the slippery ooze that now lay across the deck. With a curse he slipped and went crashing headlong into a waste receptacle. Caught in the spray of gummy waste fluid, the gleaming exterior of his stainless-steel suit was soon covered with sticky residue that clogged flexion joints and the moving parts inside them.

He still kept on coming toward Quinn, but his movements became sluggish as the damaged propulsive system of the combat rig struggled to keep pace with its command load.

"You can't continue playing tag much longer," Bruckner roared as he chased Quinn toward the far end of the chamber. "Sooner or later I'll connect. Then it's dying time, bucko."

Quinn knew Bruckner was right. There *was* no place to hide, nowhere to go. Unencumbered by the weight of any combat exoskeleton, Quinn was more mobile than Bruckner, but his antagonist had strength and staying power going for him, which tended to even things out.

Quinn backed up against a flight of steel utility stairs leading up to the catwalk encircling the enormous generator node. Nomad ducked under another swing of Bruckner's motorized, armor-encased fist and smashed a hastily grabbed dispenser jug into the side of the rogue spook's metal-cowled head.

Lubrication grease dripped down into Bruckner's unprotected eyes, temporarily blinding him, and Quinn took advantage of the seconds he'd bought with the surprise maneuver to scramble up the stairs toward the catwalk. Quickly recovering, Bruckner was up the steps after him, gaining the top of the stairwell moments after Quinn reached it. There Bruckner turned and saw Quinn make a break to the left.

Bruckner followed in a series of seven-league-boot steps, seeing Quinn stop and grab for something in the dimly lit area at one end of the bends in the square-cornered catwalk. A light flared in Quinn's hand, and in a minute Bruckner saw that it was the flame of an oxyacetylene cutting torch that Quinn had snatched up from a worktable littered with equipment used by a repair crew.

Bruckner froze in his tracks. He feared that the ultrahot torch might be effective enough to cut through the armor of his combat exoskeleton. He had to have a healthy respect for anything that was capable of slicing through construction-grade steel.

Quinn saw Bruckner hesitate for a moment and lunged at him with the oxyacetylene flame, his eyes protected by welder's goggles that he had snatched up from the table in addition to the cutting tool. Confronted with the incandescent jet from the nozzle of the torch, Bruckner lost his nerve and backed against the railing.

Quinn thrust the nozzle of the cutting torch into Bruckner's steel-clad chest. Sparks of flash-melted metal sprayed from the suit in a fiery gout.

Bruckner could feel the intense heat penetrate right through his combat armor. A yowl of pain escaped his lips as he crabbed sideways along the railing of the parapet, desperate to avoid the torch's searing flame.

"Now wait a minute, good buddy," he begged Quinn. "Maybe we can work something out, after all."

Bruckner's systems diagnostics were reporting that his suit's servomotors had been severely damaged by the heat of the oxyacetylene cutting torch. Indeed, Bruckner could feel new stiffness in his robotic legs as he continued to slide his way along the railing of the catwalk.

"I've got a better idea," Quinn retorted as he jabbed at Bruckner with the torch's cutting edge. "How about if you just die?"

Quinn lunged at Bruckner's midsection with the cutting torch flame, and Bruckner shrieked in panic and threw up his arms in a reflexive posture of submission and defense. As a result of the malfunctioning suit system, the sudden movements propelled him straight over the edge of the catwalk railing.

The five-hundred-pound combat suit plummeted directly toward the deck of the generator node. The trajectory of Bruckner's fall dropped him squarely into the row of squat waste-fluid tanks that were still gushing their oily green contents onto the deck.

Stanching the flow of gaseous fuel, Quinn threw down the spluttering torch, pulled off the mask and peered over the edge of the catwalk. The weight of Bruckner's exoskeleton had sent him crashing right through the shell of a huge chemical waste tank.

Plumes of green-black spray from the pressurized tank were leaping and dancing all around the floundering man. Bruckner's upper torso still remained outside the shell of the tank while the rest of the exoskeleton was inside, immersed in toxic slurry.

The slippery waste fluid was as good as quicksand. With each passing moment Bruckner sank deeper and deeper into the pool of highly corrosive chemical soup.

"Help me, Quinn!" he yelled, sinking lower and lower despite his violent thrashing. "I'm going down!"

Quinn watched Bruckner struggle, but there was nothing he could do even if he wanted to intervene. Like a man falling through a sheet of ice, Bruckner's torso kept slipping down and down into the tank of toxic residue.

Moments later he fell completely through the rupture in the shell as the rush of fluid gushing from the tank began to slow to a trickle. When Bruckner's head disappeared completely from view, Quinn sprinted to the other end of the catwalk and made his way down a stairwell toward the front of the generator room that hadn't been contaminated yet by the rapidly spreading film of waste slurry, still hearing the alarm Klaxons wailing in his ears.

He found an undamaged workstation, which he intended to use to key in a fast-acting "bomb" program. However, the computer screen was already issuing a warning. Bruckner's tumble into the waste receptacle had overloaded the delicately balanced waste-purification system. The computer was attempting to take emergency measures to seal off the system and had alerted technicians to the problem.

The fail-soft program that had been triggered gave Quinn a fast lane into the heart of the system that he hadn't had before. Primed for technical intervention, the computer had already opened an override cell into which an emergency code could be entered.

Instead of a code that would correct the problem, Quinn input his bomb program and set it to cause the nuclear reactor to go critical in a matter of minutes. At the same time Quinn informed the base computer that an emergency repair crew was already on the scene and to revert to normal operational status immediately, after which the system would be blocked to all access attempts. With no emergency status being signaled, the overload would continue to grow in severity.

Already the floor of the generator node was covered with steam from pressurized pipes that were beginning to reach the point of bursting. Sparks were ejected from electrical cable conduits as increased current flow caused them to overheat seriously, and the lights were dimming with power surges coursing through the circuitry.

His sabotage accomplished, Quinn raced back toward the utility elevator that provided access to the dynamo node. As he reached the elevator, he saw the level indicator above the doors blink on at the level number of the node.

The doors promptly opened, and Quinn stood face-to-face with a squad of heavily armed, gray-suited security men.

"Hell, it's about time you got down here!" Quinn yelled at them, thinking fast, gambling that his own commandeered guard uniform would continue to deceive the opposition. "I've been trying to get a line to central comm for the past fifteen minutes!''

"We received orders from—"

"I know *damn well* you received orders," Quinn snapped at the man who had spoken. "I sent them. Now get going. Search the whole damn place. The intruder is somewhere in here. He coldcocked me and took my weapon."

"You'll have to turn in a report," the cowed man called after Quinn as he strode toward the elevator car.

"I know what I have to do!" Quinn shouted back. "But first I'm heading for the infirmary. Hell, I might have a concussion here." He hit the button that set the elevator doors opening.

"All right, what are you waiting for?" the head sky soldier shouted at his crew. "Fan out and find the intruder. Hop to it."

Quinn's ploy was working. The squad of Castle guards were off and running, fanning out through the generator room as their leader watched with his SMG ported on his shoulder.

Just before he stepped into the elevator, Quinn managed to pull rank and commandeer an SMG before he left the scene. Now Quinn rode the utility elevator toward the level where the guard he'd disarmed earlier had said Ramsey was being kept.

He would find her.

30

Minutes later Quinn reached the level of Castle's D-Section node. Just as the doors of the utility elevator slid aside, he saw the overhead lights suddenly dim and felt the station shudder as a shock wave from a distant explosion made the deck sway wildly beneath his booted feet.

The sudden impact rocked Quinn on his heels as he exited the car and almost sent him sprawling. Outside in the corridor anarchy reigned.

Panic-stricken Castle personnel in their gray-and-white jumpsuits were hustling everywhere, shouting in consternation as the lights went out entirely, then snapped back to life again, dimmer than they had originally been.

Quinn made his way along the Node 5 corridor until he reached a section marked Restricted Area. Authorized Personnel Only Beyond This Point. Despite the bedlam around him, Quinn noted there were still two guards with SMGs standing at their posts. Without waiting for the skytroopers to react, Quinn triggered a chattering burst of SMG fire that dropped them both in their tracks.

Quinn frisked both takedowns and found the key on one of them. He slid the specially coded "smart card" into its wall receptacle, and the D-Section bulkhead hatch immediately slid open in response.

Beyond the bulkhead there was a narrower branch corridor running perpendicular to the main passageway. There were several steel doors lining either side of the passageway, each closely spaced with the ones adjoining it.

Cell doors without a doubt, Quinn surmised. Each door featured a Judas hole where a metal plate could be raised to allow a guard in the corridor to peer through a small window at prisoners in the cells.

The first cell in from the access door was empty. Mummified remains were shackled to a wall inside the second cage. The third was also empty.

Ramsey was inside the fourth cell.

Clothes soiled and torn, she lay in a fetal position on the bare floor against the corner of a wall. She didn't move when Quinn called her name and rapped on the door, and seemed oblivious to the chaos around her.

There was no slot for a card key and no time to be overly careful about the risks to the prisoner within, so Quinn used one of his last commandeered grenades to blow the cell door off its hinges. The explosion blasted the door inward, skewing it in its frame with one massive hinge still holding fast. Nevertheless, there was enough space for Quinn to squeeze himself through.

"You okay?" he asked, stooping to lift Ramsey's head. She stared up at him with glazed eyes that could not focus on any one point for very long. Ramsey was apparently drugged to the gills.

Grabbing her under the arm, Quinn dragged her toward the blown cell door. As they reached the outer corridor again, the station was rocked by an even stronger tremor and the lights dimmed again. When they came back on long seconds later, a whole line of security men was blocking their path through the corridor.

"Freeze!" one of them shouted at Quinn, who was already pushing Ramsey toward cover and jerking his SMG into takedown position.

Before another pulse beat could pass, Quinn sent Spectre fire blazing, salvoing the weapon one-handed before any of the guards could get off a clean shot. He dropped the soldier who had issued the command and seriously wounded the second of the three hardmen.

The third one managed to get off a quick SMG burst in answer, but Quinn had by this time unshipped a grenade from his ALICE webbing. Exploding an instant later, the bouncing ball caught the gunman in its lethal splinter zone, ending the contest. With Ramsey in tow Quinn hurried down the corridor, leaving the terminally wounded man bleeding to death on the deck.

By now the tremors that had started to rock the station were beginning to come in rapid pulses. Entire sections of the node corridor had been plunged into darkness. The station was vibrating fiercely as its joists struggled with titanic stresses.

Castle was breaking apart.

Chunks of debris were now falling from the ceiling. Cascades of hot, fiery sparks showered Quinn as circuits exploded and clouds of steam escaped from rows of conduit tubing that snaked along the corridor walls.

It wouldn't be long before the orbital station would disintegrate completely.

Quinn knew what he was searching for as he half pushed, half carried the semiconscious woman through corridors filled with acrid, choking smoke and sparks thrown off by exposed live cables. He was searching for one of the orbital reentry rescue modules, ORRMs, that were engineered into the station as orbit-to-ground lifeboats.

According to the computer plans and schematics that Quinn had uncovered during his computer hacking, there were several ORRMs located at various points along the perimeter of the space-based installation. Each escape module had room enough for only two occupants.

One module, Quinn knew, was located on the detention level of the station. When Quinn reached it with Ramsey in tow, there were two Castle troopers already there ahead of them, fighting each other to get control of the lifesaving rescue vehicle.

A third was already inside the ORRM. He had an SMG in his fist and was fixing to shoot the others, but fear of damaging the equipment in the rescue module with a poorly aimed burst prevented him from firing.

Quinn had no such problems in deploying his own commandeered SMG.

Two quick bursts neatly swept aside the guards who'd been wrestling one another. The sky-trooper inside the module angled his weapon at Quinn but realized at the last minute that he was better off simply closing the armored hatch and popping the lifeboat into space, leaving the opposition to die along with the rapidly disintegrating station.

Quinn realized what was going down as the rescue module's hatch slid closed. Moving fast, he managed to jam the SMG's muzzle between the hatch and its frame before it shut completely.

Through the narrow aperture Quinn saw a flash of gray coveralls from within the module. He risked a two-round burst and heard a muffled grunt from inside the rescue pod as fire ripped from the muzzle of the Spectre.

The hatch slid slowly open again. The bleeding soldier inside the rescue module toppled out onto the deck, his eyes staring wide open, a ragged red entry wound gaping in the center of his chest.

Quinn dragged the body from the lifeboat as yet another tremor shook the station, then pushed Ramsey inside the module. As he closed the ORRM's hatch, he heard the sounds of running feet and shouting from farther along the corridor, then saw another group of soldiers rush toward the rescue vehicle.

"Let us in, damn you!" Quinn heard a gruff voice shout, accompanied by the thudding of fists and SMG butts pounding against the hemisphere of the armored steel ORRM hull protruding into the corridor.

Quinn had no intention of opening up. He busied himself strapping Ramsey into one of the two

G-seats in the orbit-to-ground rescue vehicle, then climbed behind the module's instrumentation panel, which was undamaged by the SMG burst.

The pounding, pleading and threatening of the men out in the corridor had stopped. Now the rapid thwacks of impacting bullet rounds were heard as they fired in blind rage into the hull of the rescue module. Designed to withstand the tremendous heat and shock of atmospheric reentry, the bullets did nothing more than ricochet back at the shooters.

The command sequence for ORRM launch was designed to be self-initiating. A push of the large red button on the console started the doors closing and triggered the rescue module's jettison sequence.

JETTISONING ORBITAL REEENTRY RESCUE MODULE, flashed the message on the computer screen.

There was the steady hiss of forced-pressure oxygen flow and the staccato report of phased rocket burns, and the module lurched free of the station moorings.

Back inside the corridor the doomed Castle troopers screamed as the tremendous suction of escaping atmosphere pulled their thrashing bodies out into the frigid vacuum of space. Despite their desperate lunges for handholds, they were quickly sucked to their deaths through the opening in the hull.

As the rescue module disengaged, Quinn and Ramsey were suddenly in a state of microgravity. Quinn buckled himself into the molded G-seat as he began to float around the small spherical passenger compartment of the reentry-capable lifeboat.

REENTERING EARTH ATMOSPHERE, the computer screen flashed minutes later.

Quinn checked his wrist chronometer. Castle's nuclear core should very rapidly be reaching critical mass, he surmised. Within moments the station would explode into a million fragments as it was consumed in a nuclear fireball. If the rescue module wasn't far enough away when the nuclear blast triggered, then it would also be swept away by the burgeoning ring of scathing heat, shock waves and radiation from the exploding station.

Now the data terminal began flashing a series of numbers that listed the rate of descent of the rescue module as well as a map of the terrain below. The map showed the continental United States, and a broken arrow indicated that the ORRM's preprogrammed angle of descent would bring it down over the Pacific Northwest area, inside

Washington State. Quinn prayed that the module wouldn't land in the ocean instead.

Miles away, beyond the envelope of the earth's atmosphere, Castle exploded as its nuclear fuel supply went critical, triggering an atomic detonation. The spaceborne fireball was as intense as a miniature nova. The nuclear blast blossomed out in all directions, forming a great sphere many miles in diameter as thousands of cubic tons of structural steel was instantly vaporized in a cataclysmic blast that lit up the heavens.

The flash was visible all over the world, and electromagnetic pulses released by the orbital nuclear detonation produced massive power surges that damaged sensitive electronic equipment from Washington to Moscow.

Suddenly Quinn felt the rescue module teeter-totter with a savage lurch. The air-conditioning in the module labored to compensate for the tremendous blast of heat created by Castle's explosion.

Quinn saw the projected glide path of the buffeted ORRM shift farther east as the on-board computer calculated the new potential landing spot based on the forces of the titanic blast that had picked up the rescue module and flung it many miles off its preprogrammed trajectory.

Quinn was relieved to see that the orbit-to-ground rescue vehicle would still set down on land instead of the ocean.

MAIN DRAG CHUTES NOW DEPLOYING, the computer screen's next message flashed as the rescue module drifted down to an elevation of three thousand feet.

Plummeting earthward at hundreds of miles per second, the drag chute's sudden deployment jerked Quinn and Ramsey in their seats with a powerful tug. Had both not been strapped into their gravity-cushioned seats, they would have been knocked unconscious by the sudden, radical shift in angular momentum resulting in G-LOC or gravity-induced loss of consciousness.

LANDING SUCCESSFUL, the video terminal announced minutes later as the ORRM touched down with a massive lurch. RADIO BEACON REQUESTING ASSISTANCE OF LOCAL AUTHORITIES. PLEASE REMAIN IN ORBITAL REENTRY RESCUE MODULE IF POSSIBLE. PRESS BUTTON MARKED SURVIVAL OPTIONS IF HELP DOES NOT ARRIVE.

No thanks, Quinn thought to himself. He wasn't waiting around for more trouble to come calling. Jettisoning the hatch by hitting the black button, which blew the explosive bolts that secured it to the spherical hull of the ORRM, Quinn squinted into the mellow sunshine of a country morning.

He unstrapped Ramsey from her G-seat and pulled the still-groggy woman from the ORRM. Nearby Quinn could see a highway. He noticed that an old brick-red pickup truck had stopped short on the road and its driver was now running toward them. The man, who wore a checkered mackinaw and faded blue overalls, looked like a farmer.

"I must get to a telephone," Quinn told the man when he reached them. "I've got some important calls to make."

31

The advanced-design LHX helicraft used by the Secret Service set down on the landing pad. Nomad hopped from the passenger compartment to the ground, ducking the jet wash from the twin turbines at the rear of the fuselage.

He had just returned to Storm King Mountain from a private meeting with the President in a bugproof briefing room situated within the complex of sterile corridors that stretched beneath the White House. During this briefing Quinn had given the commander in chief a full accounting of the events leading up to his successful escape from the covert space platform....

THE PRESIDENT LOOKED like a man struck by a poleax as he listened to what the operative called Nomad had to relate. The most powerful man on earth had believed all along that Castle was an experimental station only, one devoted to secret military research and exotic weapons development projects.

The President, Quinn explained, had been cut entirely out of the loop by the circle of Daybreak conspirators. The plot engineered by Alpha had been supported by a cabal of coconspirators reaching from the lowest to the highest echelons of government. There was no other way to explain how the vast sums of money, manpower and materiel could have been diverted toward an undertaking on such a grand scale as the Castle project.

"I'll begin an immediate investigation," the President had pledged, smashing his fist angrily into his open palm. "Those responsible for this outrage won't evade the people's right to hold them accountable," he had promised.

Quinn had no doubt the President would be as good as his word. He was also well aware, however, that the full details of the Daybreak conspiracy and the Prometheus kills could never be completely made public.

One such detail concerned the female patient now undergoing therapy at the Bethesda psychiatric ward. The doctors had told Quinn that Ramsey might never regain her sanity. Alpha's drugs had left her in a vegetative state, not unconscious but with a consciousness unable to respond to reality.

Aside from spelling the end of the President's personal political future, the exposure of such a thoroughgoing conspiracy might result in widespread panic as Americans questioned the basic tenets of democratic government.

"And the identity of Alpha—you say you never got a look at him?" the President continued.

"That's right. His face and voice were both electronically cloaked."

"Amazing," the President mused. "And you were not able to confirm his death when the station blew. Is that right, too?"

"Correct, sir. For all we know, Alpha is right here in Washington at this moment, alive and well."

"Incredible, Mr. Quinn," the President exclaimed.

At that point the intercom on the President's desk beeped, and the commander in chief went around his desk to pick up the phone's handset.

"A helicopter is waiting for you," the President said, cradling the handset. "We'll continue our discussion at some later date. Right now your expertise is urgently needed to deal with STRIKE."

THE STRIKE SYSTEM had been activated by the worm program that had burrowed its way into the silicon gray matter of the Prometheus command-and-control software. The worm had to be purged from the system, rooted out immediately.

This presented several major tactical problems. The first of these concerned reaching the Cray 2010's central processing unit. The new antivirus program prepared by the CERT team was a last-ditch attempt to purge the worm. But the code could only be input directly at the computer's CPU, and therein lay the biggest problem.

With STRIKE now activated by the worm in the Cray 2010's memory bank, the knowledge-based security network was designed to present a gauntlet of death to any invader attempting to attack the CPU. The technicians had already tried to breach STRIKE's deadly security cordon by means of their remote-controlled robot drone and had failed dismally.

The only alternative at this point would be the complete shutdown of the system. The CERT team had urged the President to order a low-yield nuclear airburst as a stratagem of last resort.

The airburst would have the capability of shutting down the system by bathing the ground-based computer in electromagnetic pulses. The problem with this tactic was that the EMP that would destroy the silicon brain of the system would do so beyond all hope of recovery.

Prometheus would be destroyed beyond all possibility of salvage. Moreover, there would then be the very real likelihood that its satellite array might begin to malfunction despite Castle's destruction, fulfilling the doomsday scenario that Alpha had planned if his demands weren't met.

Quinn decided he would attempt to breach STRIKE himself in a solo penetration—one man pitting himself against the combined firepower of a dozen computer-controlled weapon systems.

Quinn knew the STRIKE system better than anyone else on earth. Its strengths and its weaknesses were a result of his own design. Quinn, and Quinn alone, could challenge the deadly gauntlet posed by STRIKE.

Unlike the walls of the command center's other passageways, the bulkheads of the corridor that gave sole access to the CPU node were fashioned from armored plate steel, far too heavy a gauge for ordinary construction purposes.

A terrorist might not pick up on this discrepancy. Nor might such an unauthorized person notice that there were no doors in the walls, no ventilation ducts, no ports of any kind whatever.

The corridor was simply a long steel tube with access possible at either end, but nowhere else.

Quinn had designed STRIKE to present initially a neutral facade to any personnel who entered the lethal corridors, luring intruders into the heart of STRIKE—its AKZ or automated killing zone—much as a Venus flytrap lures unwary insects into its jaws with the treacherous bait of easy nectar.

NOMAD STEPPED into the evenly lit sterile corridor, aware of the deadly threat that lurked just beyond its blank white walls, which were actually phased-array, sensor-laden "smart skins." Clothed in an all-black stealthsuit and wearing virtual-reality goggles strapped to his head, Quinn wielded an AUG 5.56 mm SMG as his sole item of personal armament.

The digital readout on the raster of the VRG's eyes-up display informed Quinn that elapsed mission time was ten seconds and counting.

Quinn knew what would happen next. When it did, he was ready. Massive steel plates suddenly slid down at either end of the corridor, clicking crisply into hidden mortises.

The motion of the plates was both virtually noiseless and quicksilver-swift, effectively sealing the corridor off from the rest of the underground complex. The sterile corridor had now become a potentially deadly trap.

At the same time as the plates slid down to seal off the AKZ from the rest of the Prometheus center, the corridor walls to the left and the right of Nomad rolled back into hidden receptacles in the floor of the passageway to create an empty area approximately thirty feet long by fifty feet wide— the AKZ's "containment chamber."

AUTOMATED KILLING ZONE ACTIVATED, flashed the message on the graphical display of Quinn's VRGs.

Quinn didn't need his VRGs' warning message to recognize exactly what was about to happen. After all, it had been he himself who had been the driving force behind the AKZ perimeter defense concept.

The AKZ concept was based on two principles.

The first principle was containment of the threat.

The second principle was annihilation of the threat.

Total annihilation.

These objectives were to be accomplished by shutting up the hostile forces in what was essentially a gigantic killbox. The containment chamber of the AKZ was studded everywhere by sophisticated arrays of artificial-intelligence-driven weapons.

Just like the false tunnels in the interiors of the Egyptian pyramids designed to confuse and destroy grave robbers, the access corridor to the CPU could suddenly turn into a deathtrap to wipe out terrorist assault squads. Under the annihilating saturation fire produced by the advanced weapons incorporated into the STRIKE concept, the terrorist threat would be overwhelmed by precision-targeted automatic fire, pulse laser strikes, hyperkinetic energy rounds, antiarmor submunitions and other types of lethal armament.

The levels of intense saturation fire, combined with the lightning rapidity of the firepower that could be brought to bear on intruders, was geared to tax situational awareness beyond the limits of human capability. Regardless of the nature of the threat facing the command center, the STRIKE system guaranteed that the fight would be over practically before it got started.

Quinn steeled himself for the coming onslaught, his VRGs' electronic threat sensors and finely honed combat senses working in tandem with his superbly trained physique to challenge STRIKE's AKZ and enable him to emerge unharmed at the other end of the deadly corridor.

Now the snouts of lethal weapons of automated destruction sprang from the walls and ceiling of the containment chamber. At the same time the insectlike profiles of other advanced weapons emplacements popped up from floor plates beneath the booted feet of the twenty-first-century gladiator. Sensor heads swiveled on servomechanized stalks, seeking target acquisition.

A beep sounded in Nomad's ears, signaling that his VRG confirmed target lock by the AKZ's battle-management computer system. Almost instantaneously he found himself engulfed in a storm of lethal fire.

The Automated Killing Zone was now active, white-hot as the nucleus of hell.

32

In a pulse beat the laser cannon tracked on Nomad and began firing phased bursts of its man-killing light. But the barrage of VRG-assisted AUG fire unleashed by Nomad made it through the laser's defensive shield to devastating effect.

In a whooshing fireball the armored casing of the pulse gun shattered into jagged smithereens. Once this threat was neutralized by Nomad's quick and deadly action, he rushed through the burning wreckage of the blasted weapon station.

He was by no means home free, though. The AKZ still had a world of nasty surprises in store.

Just up ahead of him high-speed coil guns firing armor-piercing hyperkinetic energy rounds popped suddenly out of the floor and ceiling. Caught in a cross-fire whirlwind of HKE rounds, Nomad tucked and rolled to evade the deadly barrage of lethal antipersonnel flechettes.

The hyperkinetic penetrator rounds had no explosive power in themselves, but they were manufactured from ultradense depleted uranium, and the energy pulses propelling them from the coil guns' muzzles with incredible speed and accuracy gave each of the HKE rounds the capability of striking a target with the impact of an exploding meteor. A single strike from one of these dartlike HKE rounds was enough to disable or kill a man.

As Nomad tucked and rolled through the eerily soundless and terrifyingly deadly coil gun barrage, he managed to take out one of the guns with a sustained AUG salvo of tumbling 5.56s. But another coil gun fired a burst at the square foot of deck space on which Quinn had just stood. The nonexplosive strike blasted a smoking crater in the two-inch-thick titanium steel floor.

Now the coil gun was already tracking around to target Nomad in its fast and lethal computerized sights. Before it could achieve target acquisition of him, Nomad raised his right arm and used the split second the gun needed to retarget and swing its barrel around to cut loose with a disabling burst of AUG fire.

The burst was accurate. Struck dead-on by the AUG's steel tumblers just as another HKE round was discharged, the sudden energy overload blasted the weapon emplacement to smithereens.

Quinn had now managed to get two-thirds of the way through the AKA, but the final third could very well claim his life. Up from the deck plates of the corridor popped a weird-looking contraption that consisted of two stainless-steel hemispheres rapidly swinging back and forth on ball bearing mounts.

The interior of the hemispheres was lined with rows of gleaming serrated cutting edges each two inches in length. The device was technically known as a nonexplosive interception antipersonnel device or NIAD. Since it was designed to operate as a shredding machine for disposable human beings, most people familiar with the device simply called it the manshredder.

The manshredder's whirling steel blades made it a highly efficient killing machine. Not only could it reduce a human being to biodegradable slush in seconds, but it was psychologically devastating on survivors witnessing what it did.

Since by the time an intruder came up against the manshredder there was nowhere else to go except back toward the devastating fire of the corridor entrance, anyone trapped in the AKZ was forced to head right into the madly spinning steel jaws of the NIAD. Quinn found himself in that position as he reached the three-quarter mark in the advanced-design gauntlet. Herded toward the manshredder by phased weapons fire, he had no other way to go except straight ahead into the gleaming steel jaws of death or back into the blazing hellzone at his back.

Quinn himself had designed it this way. Only the best and most resourceful members of any terrorist strike team could ever hope to get this far along the AKZ.

Placing such men in a no-win position—one where they were caught almost literally between a rock and a hard place—was designed to break them psychologically. Video and other sensors would indifferently record the spectacle of terrorist hitters turned into whimpering children before they were either exterminated by weapons fire or shredded by the NIAD.

Quinn knew there was a brief instant between the time when the manshredder's whirling blades passed each other during which a perfectly executed leap and tumble might get a man through the gap. While a man might theoretically jump through the aperture, computer calculations gave him only a .2 percent chance of survival.

Because the STRIKE system's automated killing zone had been designed to neutralize a strike by a terrorist group that was estimated to be between four and seven men strong, such a small risk factor was deemed acceptable. A single escapee, possibly mangled and mutilated by the whirling blades, would present little problem for security forces stationed at the other end of the death corridor.

Nomad tensed as he readied himself to take the gamble of his life. He had no choice now but to challenge the manshredder and emerge uninjured from the other side of the lethal antipersonnel device. His VRGs' targeting laser strobed, electronically painting the whirling blades and calculating the precise launch window for his leap through space. Quinn set the countdown for ten seconds.

Five . . . four . . . three . . . two . . .

Quinn took a running jump at the sound of the beep tone shrilling in his ears. As his feet left the floor, he tucked his body into a compact ball to minimize exposed body area. Executing a full three-sixty, Quinn tumbled through the centrifuging jaws of the manshredder, hearing the whoosh of wind generated by the swinging steel hemispheres.

Landing on his feet, Nomad sprinted from the corridor. He turned to see the manshredder's rapidly whirling stainless-steel jaws slow to a halt as computer sensors indicated that there were no personnel remaining in the AKZ. Moments later the manshredder sank back into the deck plates with a hydraulic whirr and disappeared.

The corridor of death was silent again.

Directly ahead, inside the Prometheus CPU node, Nomad could now see the corpse of the technician who had died when the laser pulse guns were activated by STRIKE. He was still slumped near one of the Cray 2010 instrumentation consoles.

Because STRIKE was still triggered, those laser blasters were still engaged, Quinn knew. However, their passive TI sensor heads were completely spoofed by the advanced-heat signature suppression technology of Quinn's stealthsuit.

Invisible to the sensor eyes of the ceiling-mounted lasers, Quinn raised the AUG in a two-handed grip and launched a salvo of 5.56 mm rippers at the stubby black snout of each pulse cannon, knocking them out of commission before they could even see him.

With the lasers neutralized, Quinn seated himself at one of the video display terminals of the CPU's command-and-control instrument console. The raster screen flashed instantly to life as Nomad input the activation code sequence at the terminal.

Calling up a blank data screen for the advance AMOS language that the Prometheus system's software was written in, Quinn began logging in the antiviral code he had committed to memory. When the final keystroke was entered, Quinn copied the code into the software operating system of the Cray, thereby sending his virus-killing algorithms coursing through the infected computer like a potent healing medicine.

The results were spectacular and virtually instanteous. The CPU began painting flashing patterns on the video display screen as the antiviral program started blocking off the computer's memory register addresses from control by the Daybreak virus agent.

One by one the Cray 2010's memory registers were processed and sanitized of all lingering traces of the invading code. The antiviral program then proceeded to the CMOS segment of the computer BIOS, then attacked the bugs lurking in its software operating system, its applications programs and finally its logged files.

CHECKSUM ERRORS: 0, flashed the onscreen message. SYSTEM DECONTAMINATION SUCCESSFUL.

Suddenly the grille of the commo unit on Quinn's side beeped. He picked up one of the phone handsets nearby and put it to his ear. Jack Redding was on the other end of the comm line.

"You just made a lot of people happy, Quinn," he said, the jubilation he felt evident in his voice. In the background Quinn could hear the sound of the CERT technicians wildly cheering, like a bunch of schoolkids whose team had just won the big game. "The CPU reads clean. We've got Prometheus back!"

EPILOGUE

The President of the United States stood before the burnished mahogany podium to address the United Nations General Assembly. The subject of his address was the Prometheus Net.

"Citizens of the world," the President began as he smiled into the camera lenses of the world's news media. "Today marks the beginning of a shining era where virtually limitless energy can supply mankind with clean, safe power—power derived from the light of the sun itself."

To the left and right of the President two immense video screens relayed real-time images of the satellites taken from space planes cruising in low earth orbit. Astronauts of many nations were on board the manta-ray shaped ASPs, charged with the mission of verifying the energization of the Prometheus Net. Some astronauts had gone EVA, clustering around each orbiting solar collection platform like ministering angels, subjecting each satellite to batteries of sophisticated on-site computer diagnostic checks.

"The full story of the behind-the-scenes struggle that had to be fought before Prometheus could become a reality may never be known," the President went on as his address was beamed to billions of viewers across the planet.

"We will reveal further details as they become available. All we know now is that a conspiracy to deprive humanity of this great benefit has been stamped out by the efforts of a valiant few."

A chorus of applause greeted the President's final remarks as statesmen from around the world rose from their seats and gave the American leader a standing ovation.

The President knew a great deal more about how the Prometheus project had been salvaged than he was saying. Nobody but a handful knew the complete story, and none beyond this privileged circle might ever learn the truth, but the world owed the operative known as Quinn. It owed him its future.

THE BLACK-GARBED FIGURE dragged the inflatable raft up from the waterline and hid it behind some big rocks. A black nylon watch cap covered the striker's head, and as he turned to scramble up the rise at the end of the beach zone, a shaft of moonlight lighted his face for a few brief pulse beats.

The face was a mass of scar tissue. One ear was little more than a shriveled stump, while the lower jaw was twisted all out of shape.

Only the eyes were alive.

The mad blue eyes glowed with an inner fire, the burning, seething fire of unquenchable hate.

Hate for the shadow warrior they called Nomad, hate that gnawed at Wild Bill Bruckner's soul and demanded the satisfaction that his warped psyche knew he could never obtain except by killing Quinn.

Tonight Bruckner would get the satisfaction he craved. He would pay Quinn back many times over for what had been done to him on board the covert space station.

Quinn had left him for dead, but Bruckner didn't die so easily. His combat cocoon had still been kicking as he'd slid down into the chemical waste tank. It was barely functional, but despite being encrusted with slippery toxic slime, it had still had enough wallop left in it to go the distance.

Bruckner had been able to smash his way out through the hull of the waste storage canister before the armored exoskeleton had shorted out and died on him completely. Still high on his own adrenaline and numb to the pain from the corro-

sive fluids that had eaten away his skin, Bruckner
had shucked the steel cocoon, checked a systems
control console in the generator node and seen
that Quinn had overridden the fail-soft safe-
guards preventing the nuclear furnace from exploding.

He had realized that destruction was imminent
as he had felt the entire station shudder violently.
Debris had rained down on his head, and the deck
had seesawed under his feet.

Bruckner had known then that it was too late
for anything but escape. He had found his way to
the space plane docked at the station just as the
ASP's crew was closing its boarding hatch. Despite the severe pain rocking his nervous system,
Bruckner had sworn he would get revenge on
Quinn.

Now that time had come.

Dues-paying time.

Up close and personal.

The only way that hit the sweet spot.

Bruckner crested the grassy dune beyond the
beach line and cradled the weapon he had brought
with him. The bullpup autoshotgun had a fifty-
round shell capacity in its drum magazine. Each
ball of shot would pack the equivalent firepower

of a .38-caliber round. Enough lead to put a hole where it counted.

LIKE BILLIONS of others around the world, Quinn watched on his media center as the President addressed the United Nations. Quinn had opted to bow out of the limelight and was recharging his batteries at his Chesapeake Bay hideaway.

Let the others grab the glory, was his philosophy. Quinn had never been interested in the applause, anyway. He had played his part, and the mission had been successfully concluded. That was all he cared about.

The President spoke eloquently, calling attention to the hardships of many who had risked—and in some cases sacrificed—their lives to make possible the unprecedented new energy resource for mankind.

"And now, my fellow citizens of the world," the President said, "I take pride in declaring the Prometheus Net on-line."

The monitors to either side of the President switched to cutaways of the phased-array satellite network being energized. Billions watched the great solar collection panels glowing like liquid fire as they were tilted into the sun. Quinn knew this was a sight that none would ever forget. It was truly a historic moment.

The system was working, proclaimed the spin doctors and media hacks in voice-overs after the President concluded his presentation. It was working flawlessly, they trumpeted.

Quinn knew differently, though. He knew that thanks to viral damage sustained by the system, the Prometheus network would take another decade at least to be completely repaired.

Although all of the viral data "DNA" had technically been purged from the software and hardware, there was no telling what hidden scraps of it were still lurking in the silicon, ready to replicate at any time. For that reason the system could only generate less than a quarter of the power amplitude it had been designed to yield.

An energy-hungry world would have to make do with this as best it could. Quinn figured it was at least a start. In the end it would be mankind's will to use the gift wisely that would determine the ultimate success of the Prometheus Net.

BRUCKNER CLIMBED UP the side of the house, swung onto the widow's walk and was inside in seconds through doors whose locks he'd quickly picked. The upstairs area was dark, but the lights were on below. Good. He froze in place, listening to footsteps on the stairs. Crouching near the top

Quinn mounting the stair-

kemo sabe," Bruckner rasped as he self erect, the bullpup pointed at Quinn's tion. "Didn't think you'd see your old buddy again, did you?"

"Not really," Quinn replied without flinching. "You know what they say about rotten apples, don't you, Bruckner?"

His anger at full boil, Bruckner smashed the buttstock of the bullpup across Quinn's face. The unexpected blow sent him reeling down the stairs. Bruckner bolted downward as Quinn struggled to right himself. The crazed spook swung the business end of the bullpup toward Quinn's head.

"Before you die, you bastard, I want you to see what you did to me," he growled as Quinn rose shakily to one leg beside a table with an antique hurricane lamp perched on top of it. "Look at me," he said, pulling off his watch cap. Beneath was a fused mass of bone from which all hair and much of the flesh appeared to have been singed.

Before Bruckner could trigger a put-away burst, Quinn reached out. With a sweep of his arm he flung the kerosene lamp at the intruder. The old brittle glass shattered as the flammable liquid splashed all over him. Bruckner triggered the bullpup, but he was blinded by the stinging liquid, and the burst drilled into the ceiling instead of striking its intended target.

Grabbing a propane gas lighter from the same table he'd snatched the lamp, Quinn squirted the jet of flame directly into Bruckner's face. The kerosene ignited instantly, and Bruckner was suddenly haloed in flames. The burning figure let out a demented shriek of horror. Dropping his weapon, he hurled himself through the picture window to his rear.

Quinn scooped up Bruckner's fallen bullpup and jutted the barrel out through the empty window frame, squeezing off a burst at the mass of flames that ran helter-skelter through the night.

He couldn't tell if the burst he'd fired hit Bruckner or not, but he also didn't give a damn. One way or another Taurus was broken. By dusting him Quinn would actually be doing Bruckner a favor he didn't deserve.

Quinn put down Bruckner's weapon and looked up at the sky. It was a clear, cold night, and the constellations were visible overhead.

Amid those stars Quinn thought he detected the sudden flash of a Prometheus satellite. Then he heard the muffled roar of an outboard motor above the distant crashing of the midnight surf, and knew that his covert war was just beginning.

New from Gold Eagle—the ultimate in action
adventure fiction with a time-travel twist!

TIMERAIDER

John Barnes

Dan Samson is the eternal warrior—a much
decorated Vietnam veteran who finds himself
thrown back in time to fight battles of the past.

In Book 1: WARTIDE, he's deep in the battle to
retake Italy from the Nazis. Facing the heat of
deadly firefights in a guerrilla war, Dan Samson
knows that nothing—not even his own life and
safety—can stop him from fulfilling the course
of history.

Available in April at your favorite retail outlet, or order your copy now by sending your name,
address, zip or postal code, along with a check or money order for $3.50 plus 75¢ postage
and handling ($1.00 in Canada), payable to Gold Eagle Books to:

In the U.S.

Gold Eagle Books
3010 Walden Avenue
P.O. Box 1325
Buffalo, NY 14269-1325

In Canada

Gold Eagle Books
P.O. Box 609
Fort Erie, Ontario
L2A 5X3

Please specify book title with your order.
Canadian residents add applicable federal and provincial taxes.

TR1

**Welcome to Deathlands,
where you don't have to
die to go to hell.**

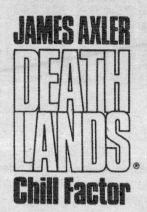

JAMES AXLER
DEATH LANDS ®
Chill Factor

Trekking through the ruins of a nuclear-devastated America, Ryan
Cawdor and his nomadic band of warrior-survivalists search for
the secrets of the past that might promise a future.

To rescue his young son enslaved in the frigid North, Ryan must
first face one of his oldest enemies—and play out the deadly fi-
nale to their private war.

Available in May at your favorite retail outlet, or order your copy by sending your name, address, zip or postal code, along with a check or money order for $4.99 plus 75¢ postage and
handling ($1.00 in Canada), payable to Gold Eagle Books to:

In the U.S.

Gold Eagle Books
3010 Walden Avenue
P.O. Box 1325
Buffalo, NY 14269-1325

In Canada

Gold Eagle Books
P.O. Box 609
Fort Erie, Ontario
L2A 5X3

Please specify book title with your order.
Canadian residents add applicable federal and provincial taxes.

DL-15

In the bestselling tradition of *ROBOCOP* and
HORN—CADE, a new series from Gold Eagle,
captures the excitement and danger of law
enforcement in the 21st century!

MIKE LINAKER

In crime-torn New York City of the 21st century, a new breed of
cop brings home the law—Justice Marshal Cade and his
cyborg partner, Janek—a steel-and-badge team that makes
the rules—and breaks them.

In Book 1: DARKSIDERS, the dynamic duo investigates the bizarre
disappearance of the Darksiders—society's outcasts, who live
below the streets of New York. The trail leads to an asteroid
mining colony where Cade must make an agonizing choice
between love and justice.

Available in May at your favorite retail outlet, or order your copy now by sending your name,
address, zip or postal code, along with a check or money order for $3.50 plus 75¢ postage
and handling ($1.00 in Canada), payable to Gold Eagle Books to:

In the U.S.

Gold Eagle Books
3010 Walden Avenue
P.O. Box 1325
Buffalo, NY 14269-1325

In Canada

Gold Eagle Books
P.O. Box 609
Fort Erie, Ontario
L2A 5X3

Please specify book title with your order.
Canadian residents add applicable federal and provincial taxes.

GOLD
EAGLE ®

CADE1R

These heroes can't be beat!
Celebrate the American hero with this collection of never-before-published installments of America's finest action teams—ABLE TEAM, PHOENIX FORCE and VIETNAM: GROUND ZERO—only in Gold Eagle's

Available for the first time in print, eight new hard-hitting and complete episodes of America's favorite heroes are contained in three action-packed volumes:

In HEROES: Book I   July $5.99   592 pages

ABLE TEAM: Razorback by Dick Stivers
PHOENIX FORCE: Survival Run by Gar Wilson
VIETNAM: GROUND ZERO: Zebra Cube by Robert Baxter

In HEROES: Book II   August $5.99   592 pages

PHOENIX FORCE: Hell Quest by Gar Wilson
ABLE TEAM: Death Lash by Dick Stivers
PHOENIX FORCE: Dirty Mission by Gar Wilson

In HEROES: Book III   September $4.99   448 pages

ABLE TEAM: Secret Justice by Dick Stivers
PHOENIX FORCE: Terror in Warsaw by Gar Wilson

Celebrate the finest hour of the American hero with your copy of the Gold Eagle HEROES collection.

Available in retail stores in the coming months.

HEROES